AMISH SPRING BLOOMS

AN AMISH ROMANCE NOVELLA

RACHEL J. GOOD

Published as "Hope Blooms" in *Amish Spring Romance*; copyright © 2022 by Rachel J. Good

ISBN: 978-1-63888-031-8 (paperback),

978-1-63888-032-5 (ebook)

CHAPTER 1

Fury in his eyes, Josiah Miller's brother burst through the door of their family home and headed straight for Josiah, waving a folded paper and an envelope. "This is all your fault," Simon screamed.

"What's my fault?" Josiah stepped back a few steps and held up a hand as his brother barreled toward him, hoping to calm Simon enough to get a coherent answer.

"This." Simon thrust the yellow stationery and envelope at Josiah, sank into the nearest chair, and buried his head in his hands. "What am I going to do?"

Josiah turned over the crumpled and smudged envelope. He could barely read the return address, but the letter had come from Bird-in-Hand, the town in Lancaster County where Simon had worked six years ago. At least he had until Josiah had intervened. The bishop had agreed with Josiah and insisted Simon move back to Gratz. No one but Josiah and the bishop knew the real reason Simon had returned to their community after only a few months at his new job.

Desperation edged Simon's voice. "I don't want Katie to find out. I never told her about this."

"You didn't?" It wasn't Josiah's place to lecture his brother, but surely a husband should have shared his past with his wife.

"I—I didn't think she'd understand. It all happened long before I met her, and I didn't want to lose her."

"Maybe you should tell her now." Josiah's sister-in-law had a sweet, loving spirit. She'd be devastated by the news, but she'd forgive Simon. And now that they were married, Katie wouldn't leave him.

"I can't. I just can't." Simon shook his bowed head. "She'd never look at me the same again."

"I'm not sure that's what matters in this situation. Something needs to be done right away. And you need to take responsibility for—"

Simon cut him off. "Easy for you to say. You're not married or even dating anyone." His voice rose. "Besides, this is all your fault. If you hadn't gone to the bishop, I would have known about this. I could have taken care of it then."

"I did what was right and best for you at the time."

"Maybe for me. But what about that?" Simon waved toward the yellow letter. "Something has to be done. I don't want to upset Katie. Not when she's carrying our first *boppli*."

This was the first Josiah had heard the news. "Congratulations."

"I can't tell her now. But this has to be fixed. Right away."

As he always did when one of his younger siblings had a problem, Josiah took over the role of their deceased parents. "I'll take care of it."

And he would. He just didn't know how.

Lily Bontrager shrugged deeper into her wool coat to ward off the chill in the spring air, but neither the jacket nor the scarf she'd tied tightly around her ears could lessen the iciness in her heart. She and *Mamm* should be out here together planting these seedlings. Lily lifted her face to the tiny sliver of sun peeking out from gray clouds, so much like the shadows hiding God's grace in her own life right now.

She squeezed her eyes shut and prayed from the depths of her soul, *Please, Lord, help me find a way to ease this grief.*

Although she accepted *Mamm*'s death as God's will, the ache inside grew stronger with each passing day. Rattling around alone in the big house, once filled with laughing, squabbling siblings and two loving parents, made Lily's loneliness even more acute. And now, she had to face spring planting without *Mamm*.

"Whatcha doing?"

The shrill question startled Lily. She turned her head and spotted two little *Englisch* girls with matching impish grins, tousled hair, and threadbare dresses that had long ago faded to pale blue. They stood a few feet away, staring curiously. They'd tromped through her previously planted rows, mashing fragile seedlings.

Lily tried not to grimace. She'd nursed those plants from seeds over the past weeks. "I'm planting tomatoes."

"No, you ain't." One twin crossed her arms and glared. "Mommy says it's bad to lie."

"'Matoes is round and red." Her sister pointed to the flat of seedlings. "Them things are green and skinny."

Hiding a smile, Lily held up the seedling she'd been about to put in the ground. "If you walk carefully without stepping on the baby plants"—she waved toward the rows between them—"I'll let you sniff this. You'll see it smells like tomatoes. After I plant it, it will get taller, and when the weather is warmer, tomatoes will grow on it.

Both girls gave her skeptical looks. Then, in unison, they shook their heads.

One sister leaned close to the other one's ear. "She's lying." Her loud whisper carried. Then she lifted her chin. "'Matoes come from the store."

"That's true. Sometimes they do. But how do tomatoes get to the store?"

The little girl's defiant look slid into a puzzled frown. Then, a moment later, she crowed triumphantly, "On trucks."

Her twin nodded. "We seen those big trucks dropping off food."

"And how do the tomatoes get on those trucks?"

"They load 'em up."

"Right." Lily had never been around children who didn't know tomatoes grew in a garden. She smiled encouragingly. "Where do the drivers get the tomatoes to put on the trucks?"

The sisters gave Lily the side eye as they put their heads together. After whispering furiously for a bit, one of them admitted, "We don't know."

"They grow from plants like these."

The twins stared at her, their expressions uncertain.

"Do you want to smell this?" Lily held out the seedling. "Just remember to watch where you walk."

With an exaggerated tiptoe, the closest girl started toward Lily.

Her sister grabbed her sleeve. "Mommy says never talk to strangers."

"We already did," her twin pointed out.

"But she could snatch us."

"I promise I won't snatch you." Where had these girls lived that they were so fearful?

Lily waited until both girls had sniffed the leaves and

declared they smelled a little bit like a tomato, before she asked her question. "Where do you live?"

"Over there." One sister waved in the direction of a rundown shack near the street, just at the edge of Lily's property.

No one had lived there for years. Did it even have heat, running water, or a toilet? "Are you sure?"

They both nodded vigorously. "We moved in yesterday," they chorused. Then they giggled.

Unsure whether or not they were telling the truth, Lily extended her hand—the one without a tomato plant in it. "That means we're neighbors. Nice to meet you. My name's Lily."

"I'm Scarlett, and this is Meryl."

Meryl elbowed her sister. "I can name my own self."

Scarlett glared at her. "It's OK to help someone."

"Not when they want to do it theirselves." Meryl turned to Lily. "We're five years old, and we're twins."

"I could tell. You look alike." Since the girls seemed to want to talk about themselves, Lily asked the question that had been nagging at her ever since they'd shown up. "So, where did you move from?"

"New York City." Once again, Scarlett jumped in first to answer.

"Mommy lost her job, and we got 'victed." Meryl seemed eager to top her sister's information.

"Eee-victed." Scarlett emphasized the beginning of the word. "That's when they throw all yer stuff out on the sidewalk."

Meryl sniffled. "Not all of it. I lost my fuzzy bunny and my baby doll and my . . ."

What had these poor girls been through? Lily's heart went out to them.

Before she could find out more, a panicked voice sliced

through the air. "Scarlett? Meryl?" The front door of the shack banged open, and a young woman raced onto the porch. She studied the fields across the street and swiveled her head to glance up and down the street.

A guilty look crossed Scarlett's face.

Meryl looked about to burst into tears. "Uh-oh, Mommy's mad."

Normally, Lily barely raised her voice, but she yelled at the top of her lungs, "Back here." She could only imagine how worried the mother must be.

The young woman whirled around, and spying her daughters, charged in their direction. "Oh, you found them." Relief oozed from her voice, and the tightness in her face relaxed . . . until her gaze settled on her daughters' muddy shoes and the path they'd traveled. "Yikes! They squished your plants."

"It's all right. I can probably replant most of them." Lily wasn't sure about that, but she wanted to lessen the mother's guilt.

"I'll pay for them as soon as I can." The woman rubbed her forehead. "Not another expense," she muttered.

Perhaps she hadn't intended anyone to hear that, but Lily couldn't help feeling sorry for this young mother. Although her strained expression made her appear older, the woman couldn't be much more than twenty-one or twenty-two. Too young to have five-year-old daughters.

"I'm Lily. It's nice to meet you. Your daughters said you just moved in."

"We did. I'm Aliyah." She wrapped an arm around each daughter. "We need to go, girls. Tell Lily you're sorry for messing up her garden."

"Where to? Back to New York?" When Aliyah shook her head, the hope in Meryl's eyes died.

"To work with me."

"Nooo." Scarlett emphasized her moan with a glum expression. "Will we have to hide again?"

Redness seeped into Aliyah's cheeks. "We'll talk about it later." She tried to herd her daughters toward the shack, but Scarlett pulled away.

"Why can't we stay here with Lily?"

Through gritted teeth, Aliyah said in a low tone, "We can't afford to pay anyone. Now let's go."

"You wouldn't have to pay me." The words jumped from Lily's mouth before she had a chance to consider them. "I'd enjoy having company. I could teach the girls to garden and—"

Aliyah waved a hand to cut her off. "Thank you for your kind offer, but we couldn't impose."

"You wouldn't be imposing. My *mamm* passed recently, so I'd be happy for company."

"It wouldn't work. I have an interview shortly. If they take me, I'll be staying and covering the night shift."

Lily had never acted impulsively, but something about these little girls called to her. "I have plenty of bedrooms. Empty bedrooms that used to belong to all my brothers and sisters. Having your girls spend the night would keep me from being lonely."

Aliyah avoided Lily's eyes. "To be honest, I don't really trust the Amish. I had a very bad experience." She kept her head lowered and nibbled on her lips. "Thanks for the offer, though."

"No, Mommy." Scarlett pulled on her mother's hand, trying to drag her back. "Please don't make us go. It ain't easy to sit for hours and not make noise."

With a sigh, Aliyah corrected her. "*Isn't.* Not *ain't.* It *isn't* easy to sit." She gave Lily an embarrassed shrug. "They picked up bad grammar in our old neighborhood. We've been working on it, but . . ."

Meryl added her plea to her sister's. "Let us stay with Lily. We'll be good."

"Why don't we try it this once?" Lily suggested.

Doubt clouded Aliyah's features. "I'm not sure."

"I've taken care of plenty of children. I have a dozen nieces and nephews of all ages. If you want references, you can check with any of the neighbors here. I babysit for them too." Lily gestured toward the houses across the street and next door.

"Please, Mommy." Meryl's eyes swam with moisture.

Maybe her daughter's tears swayed her, but each word came out reluctantly. "Just this once."

Her daughters both cheered.

She bent to look them in the eyes. "Behave yourselves and do what you're told. I'd better not hear about you causing any trouble. And do what you can to fix these broken plants." She stood and brushed off her pants. "I have to go. I don't want to be late."

Lily wanted to reassure Aliyah and remove some of the worry from her eyes. "I'll take good care of your daughters."

With a terse "thank you," Aliyah strode off.

Two eager faces smiled up at Lily. What had she gotten herself into? She'd asked God for a way to get over her grief. Perhaps this had been His answer.

CHAPTER 2

Josiah fidgeted as his driver cruised up and down the Bird-in-Hand country road printed on the envelope. The return address on his brother's envelope had been smudged, and he squinted to make out the name and house number. Four mailboxes stood together on one side of the road. That one looked the closest to the smudged number, but which house did each mailbox belong to?

"Wait," Josiah cried.

Rusty slammed on his brakes, pitching Josiah forward. The seatbelt chafed against his chest, but kept him from flying too far forward.

"Sorry," Rusty apologized. "You startled me. Did you mean for me to stop?"

"*Jah*, I did. Could you pull over somewhere near here? I want to walk along this road a ways." He'd seen a woman with two girls about the right age.

Rusty drew the car onto the opposite shoulder, and Josiah paced back down the road. It had been one of these yards along here. He passed a tiny, rundown house, and then in the spacious backyard nearby, a beautiful blonde Amish woman knelt in a garden.

At the sight of her, Josiah's heart flip-flopped. But what started his pulse racing was not the woman's beauty, but the two small girls staring up at her with enraptured faces. They seemed to be hanging on her every word. What was she saying that held such intense interest? Josiah wanted to find out, but he held himself back.

Those twins had his brother's eyes and features. Simon used to stare at Josiah with that same concentration. This had to be the right house. But Josiah had always believed Simon's ex-girlfriend was *Englisch.* Although maybe she'd been going through *Rumschpringa* too and only dressed *Englisch.* But several other things didn't add up. The letter-writer claimed to be living in poverty and asked for money. Yet, from this distance, the blonde's dress and black work apron appeared almost new. But the girls faded dresses seemed almost *Englisch* and very bedraggled. No Amish mother in his community treated herself to new clothes while making her children do without. And the girls' hair hung down uncombed instead of being pulled back in bobs. What was this mother thinking?

The garden must belong to the huge house nearby. As if to prove him right, the blonde stood, dusted off her apron, and took the girls' hands. They picked their way through the newly planted seedlings, laughing and chatting. She looked like a kind and loving mother, not one to neglect her children's hair and clothing.

The trio headed for the back porch together and entered the house before Josiah had time to decide what to do. Should he knock on the door? What would he say? He'd planned to offer the girl money, but anyone who lived in that well-maintained farmhouse didn't need it. Besides, with her being Amish, the church would help her.

Josiah went over the letter in his mind. He'd read it again when he returned to the bed-and-breakfast where he was staying. But she'd claimed the roof leaked, they had no heat, and the children were hungry. None of those fit the picture in front of him. Maybe she and the girls had found a room or two to rent in this house? If so, her circumstances weren't as dire as she'd described them.

"Excuse me. Can I help you?" An elderly Amish man hobbled in Josiah's direction. "Are you lost?"

Not exactly. Josiah shook his head and posed a question of his own. "Is tomorrow church Sunday in this *g'may*?"

"It is. You'd like to attend?"

"*Jah*, I would. Can you tell me where it will be held?"

The man introduced himself as Thomas King and gave Josiah directions. "I'll look forward to seeing you tomorrow."

"*Danke.* I'll be there." Josiah headed for the car.

That would give him a chance to study the girls more closely to be sure his eyes weren't playing tricks on him. And perhaps he could find a way to talk to their *mamm*. Or find out her true situation from others.

After they'd all cleaned up from gardening, Lily sat on the couch with her heavy encyclopedia of gardening. She flipped to the pages showing the growth of the tomato from seeds to fruit.

"I planted seeds that looked like this in small containers. I kept them warm even when it was cold outside. And they grew. Here's how tall they'll be in a few weeks."

"They grow flowers?" Scarlett narrowed her eyes. "I don't see no 'matoes."

"After the yellow flowers fall off, you can see the baby tomatoes." Lily turned the page.

Meryl shook her head. "*Unh-uh.* They's green."

"*Jah,* they are. When they turn red, they're ready to pick and eat."

Disbelief on their faces, the girls flipped the pages, studying the life cycle of the tomato plant.

Lily stood. "Why don't you look at this book while I fix us some supper?"

Scarlett looked up. "What we having?"

"Meatloaf, baked potatoes, and corn." Lily hoped the girls would like that. She wanted to fill their stomachs. They looked thin and hungry.

Evidently, she'd made a good choice. After the girls had spent more than an hour poring over the gardening book and exclaiming over oranges and lemons growing on trees and bananas growing upside down, they raced to the table and wolfed down their meals.

When Lily offered them seconds, their eyes widened.

They stayed silent for a full minute, before Meryl said in a tentative voice, "We can have more?"

"Of course. There's plenty left." Lily indicated the rest of the half-eaten meatloaf. She'd also baked extra potatoes. If the girls didn't eat them, she'd slice them for fried potatoes tomorrow.

Meryl nudged Scarlett, then leaned over to whisper in her ear. "We can sneak it in our pockets for Mommy."

Her sister nodded. "Can both of us get more?"

Lily nodded and cut generous slices of meatloaf and halved a baked potato. "This is for you to eat now. I'll wrap up the rest for your mommy."

Scarlett gasped. "All of it?"

"*Jah.* I mean *yes*. Your mom can have everything that's left."

Her eyes filled with wonder, Meryl stared at Lily. Then she breathed out a small, startled "Thank you."

Scarlett sat, her mouth gaping open, until Meryl elbowed her and hissed, "Say *thank you.*"

Her sister repeated the words, but her brow furrowed. "Is you rich?"

"No, but God has given me more than enough for myself and to help others."

"Can God give Mommy lots of money and food?"

Ach, what had she started? Lily paused to find the best answer. "I don't know God's will for your mommy, but God can do anything."

"You sure?" Scarlett tilted her head to one side and watched Lily closely as she waited for an answer.

"God can give us everything we ask for, but He doesn't always do that. Sometimes He says *no*."

Scarlett crossed her arms. "That's mean."

"No. We have to trust that God knows best. He has a good reason for whatever He does."

Meryl nodded. "Like when Mommy says 'Don't eat that, so we have some food for tomorrow.'"

Lily's heart ached. How often had these little girls gone hungry?

Her mouth full of meatloaf, Scarlett declared, "I'm going to ask God for food every day."

Lily suspected God would answer that prayer. She'd already decided not to let this family miss a meal again. She'd talk to people at church about helping too. Some of the men could fix up the shack, and the woman could make sure the children were clothed and fed. The twins might be *Englisch*, but her community would never ignore someone in need, especially not young children.

Scarlett and Meryl helped wash the dishes and clean the kitchen. Evidently, they'd done chores at home, and they seemed happy to help. They relaxed enough to chatter about their past, making Lily even more determined to change their future.

But when Lily wrapped up the food and went to place it in the refrigerator, Meryl tensed up, and Scarlett tugged at Lily's skirt.

"What about Mommy?"

"This is for her," Lily assured them. "Would you like to put it in the refrigerator at your house instead?"

Meryl bit her lip. "We ain't got no fridge."

"That's cause we got no 'lectricity."

"I don't either."

Disbelief was written on both faces.

Then, Scarlett shook her head. "You gots a fridge."

"Mine's gas-powered."

Meryl's face fell. "We ain't got gas neither."

What were they doing for heating? Lily had to get to work right away. Thank heavens, they had church tomorrow. She'd get people lined up to help immediately.

Lily placed a hand on each girl's shoulder. "I hope we can get that fixed."

"You gonna ask God to do that?" Scarlett demanded.

"I am." Lily herded them toward the stairs. "And I'll ask people I know who like to help God."

"Does you know more nice people like you?"

Before Lily could answer Scarlett, Meryl chimed in. "We knowed nice people in New York. Sometimes they gived us food. But sometimes they was hungry too. Just like us."

If I have anything to say about it, you'll never go hungry again.

After helping the girls bathe and wash their hair, Lily gave them nightgowns her nieces used when they spent the night. Then she told them Bible stories as she combed the tangles out of their hair and toweled it dry. Before she tucked them into bed, she helped them say their prayers.

Instead of getting into the bed Lily had made up for her,

Meryl climbed in with Scarlett. "I always sleep with my sister."

"It keeps us warmer," Scarlett murmured sleepily. "This bed's softer than the floor."

"Is that where you've been sleeping?" Lily couldn't keep the concern from her voice.

"We don't gots no furniture yet," Meryl explained. "Most of our stuff got all broken into pieces. Those men throwed it out in the alley."

"Once Mommy gets a job, we gonna get pretty new things. She promised."

"I see." Lily added another need to her list, which had been growing and sprouting faster than her tomato seedlings. She hoped her requests would bear as much fruit.

She stood in the doorway until the girls' breathing slowed and softened. Then, with tears in her eyes, she tucked the quilt around them.

Lily had spent so much time taking care of *Mamm* she'd never had a chance to date and marry. And now she was the *alt maedel* at the singings. All her friends had paired off, and only boys younger than her attended the singings. Perhaps God had brought these little twins into her life to fill her longing to be a mother—something that most likely would never happen.

CHAPTER 3

The next morning at dawn, the girls watched fascinated as Lily combed her long hair and pulled it back into a bob.

Scarlett rushed over when Lily finished. "Do that to me."

"And me." Meryl dogged Scarlett's heels.

Lily combed her out and then had Scarlett place her head down on the table, so Lily could do her bob. Meryl copied her sister, and soon both girls had neat bobs at the back of their heads.

"I rinsed out your dresses last night, but they aren't dry yet. Would you like to wear some of my nieces' clothes?"

"To match you?" Meryl asked shyly.

"They'd be Amish dresses." Lily led them to the closet where her young nieces stored a few things. "You can pick your favorite dress."

Meryl chose pink, while Scarlett picked blue.

Then she twirled in a circle. "*Whee*, I'm Amish."

Her sister followed her lead, and they whirled in circles until they fell onto the floor, giggling and dizzy.

Once they'd calmed down, Lily gave them warm

stockings to wear underneath their dresses. The thin ankle socks with holes they'd worn yesterday provided little protection from the chilly spring weather.

"Who'd like some breakfast?" she asked.

They both stopped clowning around and stared at her.

Scarlett found her voice first. "We got a big dinner last night."

"Mommy says if you eat lots at night, your tummy don't need food in the morning," Meryl explained in a solemn tone. "But sometimes my belly hurts."

Lily tried not to let her distress show. These poor little girls. And their mother. "At my house, we have breakfast even if we had a big supper the night before."

She fed them a hearty breakfast of sausage, eggs, and toast. Once again, they gobbled down everything on their plates as well as most of their second helpings.

Meryl pushed aside a portion of each item on her plate.

Lily disliked wasting food and always cleaned her plate. When she'd been greedy as a child, *Mamm* made her sit at the table until she'd finished every bite. But she didn't want to overstuff the girls. They probably had never had enough to eat, so they hadn't learned how much to take when food was unlimited.

She asked, "You're full?"

Meryl shook her head. "I gots to save some for Mommy."

A guilty look crossed Scarlett's face as she shoveled the last bite into her mouth. "I forgot. But she can eat the meatloaf."

"I have plenty of eggs and sausage." Lily didn't want them to worry about eating everything she served them. "I can make more for your mommy if she'd like some."

"You can?" Meryl's concerned expression relaxed into a

broad smile, and she picked up her fork and finished up everything except a piece of toast.

"You can eat the toast if you want. There's more bread on the counter."

After checking where Lily pointed, Meryl ate her toast too.

"Now it's time for dishes and chores."

While they washed up and cleaned the kitchen, Lily took care of the horse and barn. She returned to puddles on the floor, but clean plates, silverware, and counters. The twins came out to help her hitch up the horse for church.

They'd never been around a horse before, so they stood far away. And when Daisy snorted and shook her mane, they jumped back and squealed.

"She's scary." Meryl pressed her back against the barn wall.

"Not really. She's gentle. Come on over and feel how soft she is."

With a little encouragement, Scarlett ventured over to pet Daisy's nose. "It's fuzzy, Mer. Try it."

After much coaxing, Meryl let Lily carry her over. With her face buried against Lily's shoulder, Meryl allowed Lily to guide her hand to Daisy's neck. "Ooo, that feels funny." Meryl lifted her head and peeked. "She's so big."

Both girls trailed Lily as she led Daisy out into the driveway and tied the horse to a post. Lily needed to leave soon, but she hadn't asked Aliyah about taking the children to church with her.

Just then, Scarlett screamed, "Mommy!" She ran toward a shadowy figure trudging down the road.

"Wait!" Lily hurried after Scarlett. When the person bent and hugged Scarlett, Lily let out a relieved breath. Meryl joined them, and as the girls and their mother walked over to

Lily, the twins chattered away, interrupting and talking over each other.

Just before they reached Lily, Scarlett announced, "Oh, and Lily made us take baths and say our prayers."

At the word *prayers*, Aliyah's eyes hardened. "I don't want my daughters exposed to the Amish religion."

"We just thanked God for His blessings and prayed for your safety."

Aliyah shifted from one foot to the other. "I dislike—" She snapped her mouth shut. "Never mind." Her voice gruff, she added, "Thank you for thinking of me."

"How did the job go?"

"Better than in New York. Bosses and hotel guests in Pennsylvania don't seem as high pressure." Her jaw tightened, though, as she studied the dresses her daughters wore.

"I'm sorry they're in Plain clothes." Lily hadn't thought she'd offend Aliyah by lending her daughters something to wear. "I rinsed out their dresses last night, but they were still damp this morning."

Her eyes flashing lightning bolts of fury, Aliyah spit out her words. "Despite what you think, I'm perfectly capable of taking care of my daughters, and we don't need charity." She whirled around and stalked off.

The girls chased after her, but Scarlett slid to a stop, dragging Meryl back with her. "We forgot the meatloaf."

"I don't know . . ." At the girl's horrified looks, Lily swallowed what she'd planned to say: *I don't know if it'll upset your mother.* Judging from Aliyah's comments, she wouldn't appreciate her daughters bringing gifts of food, but Lily couldn't disappoint the girls. "Let's get the meal, and you can take it home."

She handed them the foil-wrapped bundles and followed

them outside. Then she kept an eye on them as they dashed across the lawn, each holding a package.

An unfamiliar buggy slowed, and the driver craned his neck to look at her and the girls. He was too far away for Lily to see his face clearly, but his scrutiny made her nervous. She crossed her arms and stared at him.

Twice in the past two days, she'd had a prickly sensation of someone watching her. But maybe he hadn't been looking at her. Had he had been studying the twins?

Her inspection must have made him nervous because he urged his horse into a trot and disappeared.

Josiah's driver, Rusty, had returned to Gratz last night to be with his family for Sunday School and church. Josiah had arranged to spend a few days here. With his assistant manager in charge, he didn't have to worry about his landscaping business. And Josiah had brought some of the more complicated designs along with him to complete.

But this morning, he needed to find a way to church. Because it was their off-Sunday, the owners of the bed-and-breakfast insisted Josiah use their buggy. Grateful for the offer, he left early so he could drive past the house he'd checked out yesterday.

As he drove past, the twins, dressed in clean, pressed Amish dresses rushed outside, each waving a foil package. Maybe yesterday they'd only been dressed in ragged clothes for gardening.

Their mother appeared on the back porch ready for church. She kept an eye on the girls as they ran toward an old shack. Maybe they were feeding a poor neighbor.

Suddenly, the woman turned his way and stared directly at him. Josiah turned his face away, so she wouldn't recognize him later in church, and clicked to the horse to make it move faster. He didn't want her to think he was stalking her.

That might be harder to accomplish than he'd expected. After the women filed into church later that morning and he'd picked the right person out in the crowd, he struggled to drag his gaze away. He couldn't let the congregation see him mooning over her like a lovesick teen.

What was wrong with him? How could he possibly be attracted to the woman who'd enticed his brother into sin? He could understand why Simon had fallen for her, but Josiah had better not make the same mistake.

With great effort, he swiveled his head and focused his full attention on the minister. The words of the sermon about avoiding temptation pierced his conscience. God must be sending him a direct message not to stray.

He limited himself to a few brief peeks during the next sermon and tried to sweep his gaze around the women's section in front of her and behind her. But somehow, she always ended up in his line of sight.

After the service and the meal, Josiah set off to find her. But whenever he strolled past the kitchen or the room where the women were eating, trying to appear casual and headed elsewhere, the young mother was always chattering to someone different. She reminded him of a gadfly, flitting about aimlessly, her mouth constantly moving.

A hand descended on his shoulder. "You having trouble finding the bathroom?" Thomas King pointed to the hallway behind them. "It's that way." The knowing look in his eyes revealed he suspected Josiah hadn't been lost.

Heat flooded Josiah's cheeks. "*Danke.*" He headed in the direction Thomas had pointed.

The elderly man chuckled. "Lily's right pretty, ain't so? But more than that, she has a good heart."

Josiah pretended not to hear those comments as he scurried down the hall.

Lily? So that's her name. Josiah hadn't been able to read the name on the envelope. There had been an *li*, but it appeared to be part of a much longer name. Maybe Lily was a nickname.

Thomas was right about Lily's beauty, but as much as Josiah was drawn to the sweetness of her features, her talkativeness turned him off. He wouldn't want to be married to a woman whose mouth ran all day long.

Married? Wait, what am I thinking? Josiah reined in his thoughts with a sharp jerk. He hadn't even met this woman yet. The last thing he wanted was to get involved with his brother's ex-girlfriend. What would Simon think if Josiah brought Lily home to meet the family? Everyone would see the twins and know the truth. Or would they suspect the children belonged to Josiah? He and Simon resembled each other.

Josiah shook his head. No matter how pretty and good-hearted Lily was, he had no interest in her other than caring for her children—his brother's children.

As he exited the bathroom, he almost plowed into her and a friend chatting in the hallway.

"You are coming to the singing early tonight, right?" the woman asked Lily.

"Of course, but I have something important to talk about now."

Both of them glanced up and nodded as he edged past, but Lily barely paused in her rapid chattering. "I started to tell you about the twins earlier. I'm really worried about them. I never want them to go hungry again." Her brows drew together.

The other woman laid a hand on Lily's arm. "Don't

worry. I'll organize a rotation of people to bring meals every day."

Hmm . . . Not only had Lily come after his brother for money, she also was begging for support from the church. Most likely, she expected Simon to send cash rather than drive all the way to Lancaster County to find her. She'd told him she didn't have enough money to feed the children, but here she was lining up others to bring meals every day. What kind of a scam was she running? He intended to find out and expose her.

CHAPTER 4

When Lily arrived home from church, Aliyah dashed out of the house. "Can I talk to you for a minute?"

"Of course, but I need to take care of my horse first. Would you like to come over for tea in half an hour?"

Aliyah shuffled her feet. "You don't have to feed me."

"It's only tea. I'm happy to share my water."

"After the way I treated you?"

Lily waved a hand. "You were upset, but that's all been forgotten. Why don't we start over as friends?"

Aliyah didn't meet her gaze. "You're as generous as my girls claimed." She pivoted and hurried off to her house. "I'll come back in half an hour," she called over her shoulder.

Sure enough, she showed up with the twins in tow. Dressed in too-short pants and tight shirts, they held the folded Amish dresses and stockings Lily had given them. They handed her the clothing and thanked her.

In her hands, Aliyah held a paper plate with four cinnamon rolls.

"Mommy got them at work," Scarlett chirped.

Meryl bounced on her toes. "They're day-old, but we can dip 'em to make 'em soft."

Aliyah's cheeks reddened to the color of ripe tomatoes. "Hush, girls." She tipped her head toward the plate. "These are to thank you for taking care of the girls. And I hope you'll accept my apology for my rudeness. You didn't deserve it after all you did for my daughters."

"Like I said before, let's forget it. Come in, so we can get to know each other. I'm glad we'll be neighbors."

After they'd all settled at the table and finished their tea and rolls, Lily beckoned to the girls and led them to the other end of the large kitchen. "I have a small cabinet here with games and toys for my nieces and nephews. You can choose whatever you'd like to play with while I talk to your mommy."

Lily returned to the table, poured herself and Aliyah another cup of tea, and then settled in to discover more about her neighbor. After answering a few questions about her own life, she turned the conversation to Aliyah, and soon the young mother was spilling her life story.

"At sixteen, I ran away from my home in Georgia, hoping to be an actress. I'd gone as far north as Lancaster when I met Simon. He was Amish, but he didn't look it. I guess he was in *Rum*-something."

"*Rumschpringa*?"

"Yes, that's it. We both got small parts in one of the Sight and Sound plays." Aliyah's starry eyes revealed her love for Simon and for acting. She sat silent for a while, staring off into the distance. Lily stayed silent, waiting to hear the rest of the story.

This time, when Aliyah picked up the thread, dark storm clouds descended over her features. "Then I found out I was expecting. I wrote Simon a letter to tell him about the baby." She ran a finger around the rim of her tea cup. "I was too embarrassed and ashamed to tell him in person. Plus, I wanted to give him some time to think about it. He'd asked me to marry him, but I told him we were too young. I hoped with the baby coming . . ."

"He didn't plan to return to the Amish?"

Aliyah shrugged. "I don't know. I guess that's what he ended up doing. When I went to the house where he was staying, the man at the door took my letter and promised to give it to Simon. The next day, I returned to talk to him, but he'd disappeared. Nobody would tell me where he went. I tried to find him, but do you know how many Millers there are?"

Hundreds or thousands. Finding Simon would be like looking for a lost quilting needle in a mountain of fabric. Often, you only found it if you got poked in the finger.

"That day," Aliyah continued, "my dreams crashed and died. I had the girls and made it to New York, but I never made it on stage." She held up her rough, chapped hands. "I spent the best years of my life cleaning toilets and scrubbing floors, trying to keep my girls fed and put a roof over their heads."

"I'm sorry." For Lily, missing out on being an actress wasn't such a bad thing. And Aliyah was still quite young, but her eyes reflected the depths of her loss.

"I even named my girls after famous actresses I admired. But I guess you already figured that out." Aliyah paused. "Or maybe you didn't. You people don't watch TV or movies, do you?" Her hollow laugh held no mirth.

"No, we don't." Lily kept her words gentle. She didn't want Aliyah to feel judged.

"I dragged my daughters with me to work all hours of the day and night. They learned to sit quietly and hide whenever my boss came around. It's no life for kids, but I did what I could until I lost my job."

"What brought you back here?"

Aliyah hung her head. "You'll probably think I'm crazy."

"I think you're a good mom who did what she needed to do to survive."

"At a house I cleaned the week before I lost my job, I saw an article about this Amish garden designer in this decorating magazine. They'd snapped a picture of him from behind, but I could see a bit of his face. He looked so much like Simon, it took my breath away. And his last name was even Miller. I asked the lady if I could keep the magazine, and she let me. When we got evicted—"

"The girls mentioned that. It must have been hard."

Aliyah winced. "I didn't mean for them to see that, but I didn't have any choice. I had nowhere to leave them."

Lily tried to imagine not having anyone to lean on. Being a part of the Amish community meant she always had someone to turn to for help.

"Anyway, I had that magazine with me. And I looked up that landscaping company. When I called and asked about Simon, an employee gave me his address." Aliyah dragged in a deep breath and lowered her gaze. "I lied about why I wanted it."

Although Lily didn't agree with lying, she understood Aliyah's desperation.

"I wrote him a letter, telling him I planned to come here. He never answered me. But I came to Lancaster. Simon and I used to meet in that shack. He said it belonged to one of his relatives, but no one ever used it anymore."

Lily suspected Simon hadn't been truthful about that. When she was young, an *Englischer* owned the farm next door. Migrant workers often stayed in the shack during the harvest. After the man died, most of the land had been sold off to developers, who'd put up new homes, but the shack had stayed empty. Lily kept that information to herself. Aliyah had enough troubles already.

"If Simon's family owns the building, then my girls should have a right to stay in it." She lifted her chin. "Besides, we won't be there long. Now that I have a job, I'll save up enough for a security deposit on an apartment."

Lily would ask Thomas King who owned the property. He'd likely know. His family had lived in this area for generations. She'd contact the owner and pay rent on the shack until Aliyah moved out. Lily never wanted the girls to be evicted again.

THE OWNER of the B and B stopped Josiah as he headed to his room after the church meal. "Since you're staying a few more days, I wondered if you'd need a buggy."

Josiah hadn't worked out his transportation issues. Hiring an *Englisch* driver when he knew nobody in the area would be difficult. "A buggy would be great. Any idea where I can rent one?"

"Our neighbor is in Pinecraft until the end of the month. I talked to his son, and you can use his *daed*'s horse and buggy if you'll care for and feed the horse. You're welcome to use our stable while you're here. I can take you over there now to pick it up, if you'd like."

"That would be wonderful. *Danke.*" He have to get used to the horse and let the horse get used to him, but that solved his problem of getting to the singing tonight. Now he just needed to handle his brother's problem.

Maybe he'd figure that out at the singing. At least he hoped he would.

THE GIRL next to Lily at the singing elbowed her and whispered, "That newcomer is really handsome."

Lily couldn't help but agree. He'd ended up directly across from her, and every time she glanced up, he was studying her, a concerned frown etched into his brow. Did he think she'd done something wrong?

Her friend leaned over again. "He can't keep his eyes off you."

She was right, but an uneasy feeling crept over Lily. Rather than the dreamy expression of a man interested in her, his gaze assessed her, judged her, found her wanting.

WHEN THEY BROKE FOR SNACKS, Josiah still hadn't figured Lily out. She seemed sweet and quiet, so unlike the busybody she'd been that morning at church. Which one was her real personality, or did she go from whirlwind to withdrawn?

A group of younger boys shoved past him to be first at the snack table. Jostling each other, they knocked into a petite girl with Down syndrome and a limp. She teetered, and Josiah dashed over to steady her, but Lily caught the girl before she fell.

"Here, Martha." Lily led her over to a nearby seat. "Why don't you sit down? I'll get you a plate?"

Martha's eyes welled with tears as she clutched her elbow. As Lily took off, Josiah reached Martha's side.

He knelt in front of her. "Did you get hurt?"

Martha nodded, and teardrops spilled onto her cheeks. "Those boys hit my arm."

"Will you let me see?"

She tipped her arm up. The collision hadn't left a mark or bruise.

"I'm sorry it hurts, but it'll be fine."

"What will be fine?" Lily stood over him, a questioning look on her face.

Josiah gulped. Being this close to her did strange things to his insides. He forced out words and hoped they made sense. "The boys bumped Martha's elbow, but it's better now. Isn't it, Martha?" He turned his attention to the young girl, hoping to get his heartbeat under control.

Martha beamed, her joy lighting her whole face. "You're nice."

"*Danke.*" He couldn't help smiling.

"No, *danke* for taking care of Martha." Lily interrupted their exchange. "That was kind of you.

He stood and brushed off his pant legs. "Anyone would have done the same."

Lily shot back. "I didn't see anyone else come to her rescue, did you?"

"*Jah*, I did."

Her eyebrows rose. "You did?"

"I certainly did." He pointed to the plate she'd held. "You did."

"Ah, you." Lily tossed her head. "Very funny." She bent and handed Martha the snacks.

"Not funny at all. Very kind."

"*Danke* for the compliment, but you would have done the same."

"How do you know that?" He flashed her a teasing grin.

"Because you did."

Her bell-like laugh strummed chords deep in his soul. "Would you like me to get you a plate?" He had to do something to take his eyes off her.

"You don't have to do that."

"I want to. Besides, I'm sure Martha would like your company. Wouldn't you, Martha?"

Martha nodded as her gaze bounced from one to the

other. "Stay with me, Lily."

"Sure." Lily didn't care if she got refreshments. She'd had plenty to eat before she came.

As soon as he walked away, she sank onto the bench next to Martha before her knees collapsed. His smile had given her heart palpitations.

Who was he? And why was he here? He didn't seem to be related to anyone at church. She'd had plenty of opportunity to ask as she'd flitted around at church that morning requesting food and clothing and help for her new neighbors.

A short while later, Martha's rescuer returned bearing two plates. He handed her one.

"I hope you like what I picked. Lily, right?"

"How do you know that?"

"Martha told me."

"I did?" Martha squeaked.

"*Ah-ha.* You called me by name earlier, Martha." Lily grinned at her, but her smile faltered as she turned to face him. "And you are?"

He gave a slight bow. "Josiah."

"No last name?"

"Miller. But there are plenty of people with that name."

Maybe so. But none that looked like him or made her pulse pitter-patter like this.

"And do you have a last name, Lily?"

"Bontrager."

"Mine's Troyer," Martha told him.

"Nice to meet you, Martha Troyer, and you too, Lily Bontrager."

"Nice to meet you too, Josiah Miller."

CHAPTER 5

Lily's sassy tone made him smile. If he wasn't careful, though, he could easily end up falling for her.

"Time for more singing," someone announced.

Neither of them had eaten anything from their plates. But good thing they had to get back to singing before he made a fool of himself. Lily and Martha stayed where they were, so the girls on the other side of the table rearranged themselves. Now that Lily wasn't across from him, Josiah had trouble sneaking peeks at her.

During the next hymn, he decided the only way to find out more about Lily and the twins was to drive her home after the singing. Would she go with him?

As soon as the last song ended, he rushed over to her side of the table. "Could I drive you home?"

"Me?" Martha squealed.

"Of course," Josiah said smoothly. "Why don't you get your coat?"

Martha rushed across the room, yelling at a young man who must be her brother, "I have a ride home after the singing."

He frowned. "With who?"

Martha took his hand and dragged him over. "With Josiah."

"Um, I don't think . . ." Her brother gave Josiah an apologetic smile.

"It's all right. I invited her."

He studied Josiah suspiciously. "You did?"

"*Jah*, if Lily doesn't mind coming along to show me the directions. I'm new here." He turned to Lily and quirked an eyebrow.

She weighed the suggestion for a few moments. "I guess I could do that."

"Martha," her brother whispered, "this is just as friends."

"I know, I know. Josiah is a good friend. He's very nice." She leaned over and whispered in a voice that carried, "I think he wants to be Lily's boyfriend. He looks at her all the time."

Ach! Had he been that obvious? Josiah's face burned hotter than the crackling logs in the nearby fireplace.

Lily laughed uncomfortably. "I'd better get my coat. And I'll need to let Esther know I won't be riding home with them."

Josiah went to find his coat too. Then he escorted Martha and Lily outside. Martha sat up front, and when she got home, she begged Lily to walk her to the door.

"I think he likes you lots." Martha's words reached Josiah's ears. "Maybe you'll get married."

Josiah shook his head. Absolutely not. It surprised him a girl as lovely as Lily had never married. But then he reminded himself about why he was here. How many Amish men would want to marry a woman who'd had children out of wedlock? Even if she was gorgeous and kind and . . .

Stop right there!

No matter how appealing Lily was, Josiah had only one thing in mind tonight—finding out about the twins.

~

LILY CRINGED when Martha announced Josiah wanted to be her boyfriend. Even worse, Martha had mentioned marriage. Lily only hoped he hadn't overheard. And even more, she prayed he couldn't tell how her heart sped up around him.

He'd asked to drive her home. That had to mean something, didn't it? Usually, couples got to know each other first. But she and Josiah had managed to have a fun conversation because of Martha. And Lily admired how he'd jumped right in to help Martha.

"He's nice, isn't he?" Martha asked as she reached her front porch.

"Very nice."

Martha's lips stretched into an even wider smile. "Can I be your sidesitter?"

"Of course. If I ever get married."

"You will. Josiah really likes you." Martha opened the door and went inside, leaving Lily standing on the steps, stunned and embarrassed.

If Josiah had overheard this conversation, what would he think?

She wished she could walk home instead of having to get back in the buggy. Her steps slowed as she neared the passenger side. But Josiah's friendly smile calmed her nerves.

Martha might be right. He did seem to like her. That made her spirits sing a joyous chorus. Maybe God had brought someone into her life after all. Maybe she wouldn't have to live alone. She tried not to get her hopes up, but having someone to date would be a special blessing.

Those thoughts made her so tongue-tied, she couldn't come up with any conversation. Martha had kept the talk lively. Now that she was gone, though, Lily wanted to retreat into her shell. She couldn't do that. Not when she needed to make a good impression on the first man she'd ever been out with. But what could she say?

Josiah waited until the horse had moved away from the curb and into traffic to ask for directions to Lily's house. He already knew how to get there, but he didn't want her to know he'd driven by her house. Twice, in fact.

After she'd gotten him onto the main road, he racked his brain for a way to ask her about the twins. He couldn't just come out and say, *Tell me about your twins*. Or she'd know he'd been checking her out.

"So, do you have any children?" he blurted out the question so abruptly, she stared at him as if he were crazy. He should have found a less offensive way to phrase that.

"Me?" She gave him a puzzled look, then her face cleared. "Oh, you mean in my family?"

Of course, he meant in her family. Where else would her children be?

"I have three older brothers and two younger sisters. *Daed* died when we were younger, but *Mamm* died a few months ago."

"I'm sorry to hear that."

"*Danke.* It's been a hard adjustment. I took care of her for more than a year, and so much of my time revolved around her needs, I'm still trying to fill all the empty spots in my days." A shadow crossed her face, and she swallowed hard.

Josiah understood how much it hurt to lose a parent. "It takes a while. Give yourself time."

"You're right. I've been praying for different things to do. That's helped." She turned to him. "Tell me about your family."

This conversation had gotten way off track. When he'd asked if she had children, she'd changed that to children in her family. That hadn't been what he was asking. Had she deliberately avoided the question?

She was looking at him as if expecting an answer. *Oh, right.* She'd asked about his family.

"Not much to tell. My parents died when I was eighteen. Being the oldest, I raised my younger brother and two younger sisters. They're all grown and married now."

"But you aren't?"

Wasn't that obvious? "*Nay*, I'm not." How could he get back to the twins? "When I asked about children, I meant did you have any children of your own."

Lily gaped at him. "If I did, why would I be at the singing?"

"Because you're unmarried?" Interesting. She didn't deny having children. Instead, she'd asked a question.

"*Jah*, I am." Hurt flared in her eyes.

He hadn't meant to make her feel bad or ashamed. So far, he'd reminded her of her mother's passing and brought up her single state. Maybe he should stop avoiding his real question. "I couldn't help hearing you talk about your twins to people at church today."

"*My* twins? *Nay*, they're not mine. I'm concerned about a neighbor's children."

What? He'd offered her a ride home because he'd believed she was Simon's ex-girlfriend and planned to talk about why she needed money for the twins. Now, he couldn't do that. But he might get some information about them.

"You seemed really concerned about these twins. Can you tell me about them?"

"It's heartbreaking. I only met them yesterday, but God has been leading me to take care of them. Their mother is having trouble providing for them, but she's proud and doesn't like to accept help."

That didn't match with the letter she sent to his brother, imploring him to send her money.

Lily described the twin's reactions to meals. "I can't even imagine what their lives have been like. Going to bed hungry or skipping meals. Saving a portion of their food so their mother doesn't starve. No child should have to live that way."

A sick feeling roiled Josiah's gut. These were his brother's little ones. Simon should have been taking care of them. That poor mother. "I hate to think about what they've lived through."

"Me too. The little girls told me about being evicted, seeing their furniture and things thrown out into the street after their mother lost her job. Little Meryl never got her stuffed bunny or some of her other toys back. You should have seen her face when she told me that." Tears sprang to Lily's eyes.

Josiah wanted to reach out to comfort her, but he clenched one hand in his lap and the other on the reins. "Those poor girls."

Even as Josiah said the words, they bounced back and stabbed him straight through the heart. He owned most of that responsibility. He could have checked on Simon's girlfriend over the years. But he hadn't known she was expecting.

Lily kept talking. "*Jah*, the twins have had a rough time. And their mother has been through a lot in her young life. The father of her babies abandoned her."

"Maybe he didn't know about them." Simon had been shocked to learn he had children. If he'd known, he would have taken responsibility.

Lily shook her head. "That's the saddest part. She wrote her boyfriend a letter letting him know and dropped it off at the house where he lived. When she went back the next day, he'd disappeared. He just took off without telling her or giving her any way to contact him. I don't understand how any man could be that cruel, that uncaring."

The nausea swirling in Josiah's stomach traveled to his throat. He swallowed down the bile. He could understand it. Simon had never known.

Josiah had gotten that letter telling about the babies. Afraid Simon might go back to the girl, Josiah had hidden that letter from his brother. He'd torn it into tiny pieces and thrown away. Neither he nor Simon had ever read it.

Everything those little girls suffered over the years has been my fault.

CHAPTER 6

Lily regretted going into the graphic details. Josiah's pale face and haunted eyes showed how seriously he took this situation.

"Are you all right?" she asked in alarm.

Josiah didn't answer. He stared straight ahead as if he hadn't heard her, as if he were a million miles away, as if he were reliving all the pain the girls had gone through.

She wanted to comfort him. "Try not to dwell on the past."

His head whipped around, and he stared at her. "How did you guess?"

"From your expression." Lily reached out and laid a hand on his arm. He flinched, and she withdrew it. "We didn't know, so all we can do is make it right from now on."

"I will do that," he said with such fierceness it almost frightened her. "What can I do?"

"The church is helping. They'll provide meals. And a few contractors will renovate the shack to add heat, electricity, and running water."

"The mother and children don't have that? How can

they live there during this cold snap? The temperatures drop at night."

"I know. I dropped off some quilts, and the owner of Allgyer's Hardware promised to leave a space heater on the porch. Aliyah doesn't want charity, but if she doesn't see the giver, she can't reject the gift. At least, I hope she won't."

"What if she does?"

"She might deny herself, but she cares too much about her daughters to make them do without."

"You're sure?"

"I can't be positive. Maybe we should pray."

"Good idea."

Josiah closed his eyes briefly, but even after he opened them to concentrate on the road, his lips moved silently. What arrested Lily's attention, though, was his fervent expression. He really seemed to care about this family's needs.

Once again, her pulse fluttered. How had she been so lucky to get asked out by a man with such a loving heart? Lily bowed her head and thanked God for bringing Josiah into her life. She also prayed the two of them could work together to help Aliyah and the twins.

Josiah's thoughts pinwheeled out of control. What was he going to do? How could he make up for his past mistake? He'd doomed Simon's girlfriend and her children to a tragic life. He could take care of them now, but how could he ever erase the pain he'd caused?

Lily lifted her head after praying and flashed him the most beautiful smile. Her angelic face and expression twisted the sharp edge of guilt even deeper into his heart.

"Maybe we could work together on this?"

He sucked in a breath at her sweet trusting question and innocent eyes. She gazed at him as if . . . *Ach, no!* She didn't think he'd offered to drive her home because he wanted to court her, did she?

Her shining eyes dimmed when he didn't respond right away. Her full lower lip trembled.

Why did she have to be so appealing? So kind and caring? So . . . so . . .

How could he say *nay*? She ducked her head and looked on the verge of tears. He didn't want to hurt her again or make her cry.

Josiah cleared his throat and, against his better judgment, said, "Let's do that."

After all, she didn't need to know about his connection to the twins' difficulties. Neither did Aliyah. As Lily had counseled earlier, he wouldn't dwell on the past. Maybe he didn't need to mention his brother. No one here knew about that situation. No one but Aliyah, and he didn't need to meet her to assist with Lily's plans.

Although his conscience nagged at him, he pushed away those warnings. And he ignored the alarm bells cautioning him he'd be leading Lily on when he had no intention of offering her a relationship. No way could he risk losing his heart to Aliyah's neighbor.

LILY TURNED TO JOSIAH, startled that he'd turned in the right direction at the crossroads. "You turned here without asking." Maybe they'd become so tuned to each other's thoughts, Josiah had picked up on hers.

He shifted in the seat and tugged at his collar. "I, um, did it without thinking."

She hadn't meant to make him nervous or embarrassed.

"Don't worry," she reassured him. "You're going the right way."

He breathed out a relieved sigh. "That's, um, good."

"I'll try to pay more attention to the road." Lily wanted to clap a hand over her mouth. Why had she blurted that out? Now he'd know she'd been watching him instead. She didn't want him to think she was too forward. "I mean, our conversation has been so interesting."

Josiah cleared his throat. His answer came out rather choked. "I agree."

Ach, he really did care deeply about others.

"When you come to the next stop sign—it's about half a mile from here—you'll turn left on my road."

"All right."

Had a chill entered his voice, or was she imagining it? Maybe he regretted the trip ending so soon. She certainly did. But they'd have plenty of time to get to know each other as they helped Aliyah.

Lily wanted to dance with joy. Josiah had sneaked peeks at her during the singing and whenever he wasn't absorbed in watching the road or worrying about Aliyah and the girls. Not only did he seem interested in her, but he also wanted to care for the twins.

They may have started their relationship as almost strangers, but this would give them plenty of time to get to know each other better. Lily didn't have to spend more time with him, though, to know he had a good heart. First, he'd been kind to Martha—even driving her home—and then, he'd been deeply affected by Aliyah's plight. His goodness, generosity, and faith shone through his actions. What more could she ask in the man she hoped to court?

Martha's comment about marriage rang in Lily's ears. Courtship often led to marriage. Although it was much too early to be thinking about weddings, little trills filled her soul in anticipation of the future.

JOSIAH COULDN'T BELIEVE he'd turned toward her house without asking. Finding out the truth about Aliyah and Simon's girls had distracted him. So had being in the buggy with Lily. Her presence had totally disrupted his life.

If only he could stay here and court her . . . But that was much too dangerous. Sooner or later, he might run into Aliyah. Would she recognize him? What if Lily heard more of Aliyah's stories and figured out Josiah was related to Simon?

He'd been so lost in thought, Lily's soft question startled him.

"How long have you been in the area?" She gazed at him expectantly, as if she couldn't wait to hear his answer. He'd never been around a woman who seemed so attuned to others like this. Or maybe he'd never been close enough to find out.

Josiah answered with the truth. "Two days."

Lily sucked in a breath. "Only two days?"

"Where are you living?" When he hesitated, she nibbled at her lower lip. "Sorry if that sounded nosy. You don't have to answer, if you don't want to."

"It's all right. I'm at Miller's Bed and Breakfast."

"The one out toward the highway?"

At his *jah*, she nodded. Then she shot off another question. "Are they relatives of yours?"

His laugh came out strained. "Not that I know of."

"But why didn't you go to their church?" Lily clapped a hand over her mouth. "That's none of my business."

"This is their off-Sunday. I really wanted to go to church."

"What brought you to Lancaster?"

Josiah swallowed hard. Lies floated to mind, but he didn't want to add to his earlier dishonesty. He should just admit the truth and lift the heavy burden on his soul. But he liked how Lily gazed at him with admiration in her eyes. A man could get used to that. He mentally shook himself. If he told her he'd been the one who'd caused Aliyah's suffering, she'd never look at him that way again.

"I, um . . ." He hesitated. "Business," he hedged.

"Oh, what business are you in?"

Answering that wouldn't get him in trouble. "I own a landscaping company."

"And you think the Lancaster area will be better for business? Where were you before?"

"I'm from Gratz." Although he spoke the truth, his answer implied he'd moved to Lancaster. He needed to stop Lily's line of questioning before he told any more half-truths. "Have you lived here all your life?"

"I have." Her gentle smile revealed her fondness for her home. "I still live in the house I grew up in. I was the youngest and the only one not married when *Mamm* passed away. My brothers and sisters already had houses and farms, so they let me stay."

"That's nice." So, that large house belonged to her.

"What about you? Did you always live in Gratz?"

Why did she turn every question around, cornering him?

"I stayed in the house after my parents died. That let me keep the whole family together." Before she could ask anything else, he pulled up to the stop sign. "This is where I turn?"

"*Jah.*" She waved in the direction he'd planned to go. "I'll let you know when we get to the next turn."

He smiled at her. A big mistake. Their eyes met and held. Next thing he knew, he was drowning in depths of soft green framed by sweeps of long eyelashes. If a car hadn't pulled up behind them, he might have stayed stuck in that spot all night.

CHAPTER 7

Josiah waited for Lily to get in the house before he turned the buggy around in her driveway. He planned to pause beside that small shack.

Were they actually living in that rundown building? His stomach twisted. The blame for this lay with him—and him alone.

A small girl darted from the doorway. "Lily," she yelled, "can we stay with you tonight?"

Lily had been closing the door. She opened it wide and beamed at the child. Not just any child. His brother's daughter. His niece.

Their family should have been taking care of this little one. And her twin. And their *mamm*.

"Of course, Scarlett. Where's Meryl?"

Out of breath, the little girl panted. "She's coming."

Scarlett? Meryl? What odd names for Simon's children. Josiah didn't know any *Englischers* with those names, and he'd spent plenty of time around them when he designed their gardens.

The other twin flew across the lawn hugging her arms

around herself. Her too tight top barely reached her middle. Like her sister's shirt, the fabric had frayed from many washings. They'd both outgrown their sweatpants, leaving their bare ankles exposed to the chilly weather. Neither of them wore jackets.

The one Lily had called Scarlett stood shivering on the porch until her sister caught up with her, despite Lily's insistence she come in. When Meryl reached the porch, Scarlett put an arm around her sister and urged her through the door first.

Those two girls needed warm clothes and spring jackets right away. He couldn't do it tonight because stores had closed. Besides, he'd never shop on a Sunday. But first thing tomorrow morning, he'd see to it.

So far, the girls' mother hadn't appeared. Josiah needed to let Lily know his plan. He'd risk Aliyah seeing him, but he had to take a chance.

He hopped out of the buggy and hooked his horse to the nearby hitching post. He headed for the back porch. With Aliyah's house near the front of the property line, he hoped to stay out of sight.

After knocking, he bounced from one foot to the other, praying Lily would come quickly. The longer he stood here, the more likely Aliyah was to glance out the window or come after the girls.

Lily answered, and her eyes widened. "Josiah?" The surprise in her eyes softened into pleasure—and an invitation to enter. She held open the door.

He stepped inside. "Listen, I saw the twins run over here. I'm worried they aren't dressed warmly enough for the weather. Tomorrow morning, I'd like to take them to the store to get clothes, jackets, and shoes."

She sucked in a breath. "That's so kind of you."

The hero-worship in her eyes made him sick. If only she knew the truth. . .

"I, um, don't know much about buying girls' clothes, so if you could come along?" He left the question hanging, hoping her answer would be *jah*.

"Of course. I'd be happy to." Her bubbly, enthusiastic response and the stars shining in her eyes made it clear she'd mistaken his invitation for a date.

He didn't want more guilt added to the burden already on his conscience. "Will tomorrow at nine work?"

At his clipped words, her lips slipped from a wide, generous welcome to a *just-acquaintances* smile. He regretted his curt tone because it hurt her and also because he missed her beaming expression and the admiring looks she'd directed his way.

To prevent himself from trying to bring the spotlight of attention back in his direction, he focused on the neat mudroom. The only thing out of place were four worn shoes, one with the sole completely worn through, lying tumbled on the floor. "Where are the twins?"

Lily laughed, and the melodious sound filled him with longing—for a home, a wife, and a family. He concentrated on the shoe with the hole. Dreams of the future wouldn't be found here.

"Can't you hear them upstairs?"

Josiah had been concentrating so hard on not getting lured in by Lily's sweetness and beauty, he'd missed the scuffling and giggling overhead.

"I told them to put on my nieces' dresses, tights, and sweaters so they'd be warmer. I'll make sure they change out of them before they go home tomorrow. It'll be *wunderbar* for them to have some warm *Englisch* clothes to wear home." She smiled up at him shyly, adoringly.

Josiah's heartbeat galloped like a runaway horse. He

drew in a long, slow breath, attempting to rein in his thundering pulse.

Lily's forehead creased into a concerned frown. At first, he assumed she'd noticed his reaction to her, but she went back to talking about the twins and their mother. "Aliyah wouldn't be happy to know her daughters are wearing Plain dresses. She can't stand Amish clothes. Or people."

Lily's words washed over Josiah like a sudden dousing from a freezing hose. He'd caused that.

"I hope she'll change her mind after she gets to know us. Meanwhile, I'm trying to show her God's love."

If anyone could do that, Lily could.

An explosive *One, two, three* came from above, and the girls ricocheted down the stairs.

"I was first."

"*Nuhn-uh*. I beat you. Race you to the kitchen. One, two, three."

The twins burst into the kitchen and skidded to a stop. Josiah's rapid pulse went careening in the opposite direction as he and the five-year-olds locked gazes.

"Who are you?" the winner demanded. The rebellious thrust of her chin and her suspicious squint were a mirror image of her dad's childhood reaction to strangers.

Josiah's eyes stung. For five whole years, he'd denied these little ones time with their father, grandparents, and extended family. He'd also been responsible for their poverty.

When he didn't answer, the miniature copycat of her dad thrust her hands on hips. "I'm Scarlett, and this is Meryl."

From Meryl's pout, she didn't appreciate her sister introducing her. Or maybe losing the race had upset her. But she echoed her sister's question. "Who is you?" She studied him.

"I'm Josiah." He hoped they wouldn't recognize his

name. Had Aliyah told them about their father? Luckily, neither girl showed any sign of recognition.

A loud pounding on the front door startled all of them.

Scarlett's triumphant grin disappeared. "Oh, no. Bet that's Mommy."

Meryl sucked on her forefinger. "She said it ain't nice to ask to stay here again."

Ach! Josiah's own internal warning kicked into high gear. "I need to go. See you tomorrow morning."

Could he sneak out without Aliyah seeing him?

Lily didn't even get to say goodbye to Josiah because he rushed away so fast. She hurried to answer Aliyah's battering at the door. Lily had hoped to introduce him to Aliyah, so he could meet the person he'd be helping.

But maybe Lily's reaction to him had made him eager to leave. After she'd let her attraction to him show on her face, he'd become stiff and standoffish.

She pulled open the front door. "Hello, Aliyah. Come in."

"No, thank you. I just came to get my girls."

Scarlett and Meryl hid behind Lily's skirt as best they could, but Aliyah's eyes narrowed. Too late, Lily realized the girls had on Amish clothes.

"I told you I didn't want my children exposed to Amish ways." Aliyah glared at Lily.

"I'm so sorry. They looked chilly. I only wanted to warm them up."

"Are you implying that I don't take care of my children?"

"No, of course not."

"Let's go, girls. Get back into your own clothes. I don't have time. I'm going to be late for work."

"They're welcome to stay here again," Lily offered.

"I already told them it isn't polite to ask. They sneaked off while I was bathing."

"I'm glad to know you have water." Lily had expected the shack to have no plumbing.

"We gots to get it at the pump," Meryl volunteered. Despite her mother's scowl and signal to shush, Meryl added, "It's freezing cold." She shivered.

"*Ach*, I'm so sorry. You're welcome to use my bathroom and shower."

Aliyah stuck her nose in the air. "It's only temporary until we get an apartment."

"I understand. It doesn't make sense to hook up plumbing when you don't plan to stay long."

"That's right." Aliyah's face relaxed.

"I'd do the same for any of my neighbors. Please come over any time."

Scarlett sent her mother a pleading look. "Lily's bathroom ain't stinky like the outhouse."

Lily swallowed back a gasp. They were using the old outhouse near the woods? She thought it had been padlocked years ago.

Red crept into Aliyah's cheeks. "Time to go."

"Please let them stay. We had so much fun together last night. And they kept me from being lonely. They're such a blessing."

"A blessing? Humph. Wish they were that for me."

"Please, Mommy? Pretty please?"

"Oh, all right. If you're sure they're no bother?"

"I love having them."

"Be good," she warned her daughters.

Both of them let out loud, relieved sighs when their mother turned to leave.

"We going have fun, ain't we, Lily?" Meryl sidled up to her, and Lily put an arm around the small girl's shoulder.

"We are." Having the girls here would keep her mind off the mistakes she'd made with Josiah. She only hoped she could fix them tomorrow.

~

JOSIAH DASHED out the back door. Feeling like a fool, he flattened himself against the side of the house so Aliyah couldn't see him through the kitchen window. Would she recognize him? He couldn't take that chance. He had to get out of here without her spotting him. He jogged to his buggy and kept his face averted as his horse trotted down the driveway.

But he couldn't resist one brief glance in her direction as the buggy turned onto the road. He might have known her face, but from the back, her red hair surprised him.

Five years ago, her hair had been a ghastly shade of purple. Why she'd want to cover up the auburn hair God had given her, he'd never understand. At least, she'd gone back to her natural color. He hoped she no longer had piercings in her eyebrows, nose, and lips. The thought of rings through those delicate body parts had turned his stomach the day he'd met her, so he hadn't looked at her closely back then. Plus, he'd been trying to get rid of her before Simon discovered she'd come to visit.

Now, though, that memory made him sick. He'd answered the door, grabbed the letter, thanked her, and slammed the door shut. He'd just let out a major sigh of relief that he'd accomplished his mission when Simon rushed into the room.

"Who was at the door?"

It was the first and only time Josiah had ever deliberately lied. "A delivery person."

Simon glanced at him askance, and Josiah almost—almost—broke down and confessed. With the letter still dangling from two fingers behind his back, Josiah reminded himself his brother's soul was more important than any message the *Englischer* had delivered.

For all Josiah knew, this girl might convince Simon to stay in Bird-in-Hand. That would never do. Josiah had promised to bring his brother home, to get him out of this life of sin.

And he'd done exactly that. He waited until Simon left the room for his suitcase. Then Josiah ripped the letter to shreds and buried it under garbage in the trash can. Less than an hour later, the driver drove him and his sullen brother home to Upper Dauphin County.

After talking with the bishop, Simon confessed what he'd done and agreed to start baptismal classes when they began the following year. He'd started taking Katie out several months after they both had been baptized, and the family never brought up Simon's past again.

Josiah had put that purple-haired girl out of his mind long ago. Until that letter came. Now, though, no matter what he did, no matter how much he gave, he could never make up for the harm he'd caused. Aliyah and the twins would haunt his dreams forever.

CHAPTER 8

Josiah tossed and turned all night. As he'd expected, his past and present responsibilities kept him awake, but so did a petite blonde with an enticing smile. He welcomed the dawn with gratitude. Today, he could put things to right. And as soon as he'd done that, he'd hurry home.

When he reached Lily's house a little before nine, the girls had their noses pressed against the window pane.

Scarlett flung open the front door. "That man's here."

Josiah smiled. "Ready to go shopping?"

She nodded and pranced out the door. Meryl trailed behind.

"We gonna ride in that?" Scarlett pointed to the buggy.

"*Jah*, I mean, yes. You'd better get your jackets first."

"We don't have no coats."

"Didn't you need jackets in New York?"

Scarlett's head swished back and forth. "Mommy din't let us go outside."

"But we was still cold." Meryl shivered, and her large brown eyes, so like Simon's, flashed with remembered pain.

Each word they spoke lashed Josiah's conscience. How could he ever make this up to them?

"Meryl? Scarlett?" Lily's worried voice floated out to them.

"They're here," Josiah called, "but they don't have jackets." He reached into the buggy and brought out blankets to wrap around them.

He tucked a blanket around Meryl and lifted her into the backseat of the buggy. The little girl squealed with delight. Josiah wanted to hug her. She reminded him so much of his youngest sister when she was small. But to them, he was still a stranger.

Josiah snuggled Scarlett in beside Meryl and turned to find Lily standing on the doorstep, holding two sweaters. He melted at the tenderness in her eyes. How could he leave her and these little ones to return home?

LILY'S HEART swelled at Josiah's gentleness with the girls. He'd make a *wunderbar daed*. "I brought sweaters, but I think they'll be snug all wrapped up like that."

"Hard to believe they don't have jackets. Let's get those first before we do the rest of the shopping."

The twins squealed as Josiah flicked the reins and the horse started off.

Meryl clung to Scarlett. "It's noisy and bouncy."

"Not as noisy as a train." Scarlett leaned forward. "Is this like them rollercoasters? I ain't never been on one, but on TV they makes people scream."

"I've never ridden one either." And Lily had no desire to.

Riding in the buggy excited the girls, but it couldn't compare to shopping. Wide-eyed, the girls stared at the racks of clothing in the children's department of the large department store.

Scarlett tilted her head and gave Josiah the side-eye. "We each get one jacket? Any one we wants?"

"That's right. Pick your favorite."

She squinted at him. "Where we get the money?" She planted her hands on her hips. "We ain't gonna steal them."

"Don't worry. I'm paying."

"You sure?" Meryl looked him up and down as if to be sure he was telling the truth. "You got lots of money?"

"It's all right," Lily assured Meryl. "Josiah also plans to get you some clothes. He has enough to pay for everything." At least she hoped he did. He had offered, after all. If he didn't, she take care of the rest of the bill.

In less than an hour, Lily had helped the girls select five new outfits each, a pair of sneakers, and a jacket. Their eyes sparkled with awe as they slipped on new clothes, shoes, and their coats in the spacious restroom. Then, clutching large bags to their chests, they skipped out to the buggy.

After she settled in the back seat, Meryl ran her hand over the fuzzy sleeve of her jacket. "They ain't got nothin' this good at the thrift shop."

"I have one more place to go before we head home." Josiah pulled into the parking lot of a bank. "We should get your mommy a present too." He returned clutching a checkbook that he handed to Lily. "This might help Aliyah rent an apartment and take care of some expenses."

Lily couldn't believe his generosity. And it didn't end there. He stopped at the pretzel shop and bought each of them a warm soft pretzel. As their eyes met over the girls' heads, Lily let hers thank him for all he'd done.

Sparks flew between them, and Josiah's tender smile lit a flame inside Lily. She'd never been so attracted to a man as she was to him. She poured her deepest emotions and gratitude into the looks she sent him. His gazes returned those feelings. Hope blossomed anew in her soul.

Scarlett tugged at Josiah's hand. He bent down to her eyelevel, and she threw her arms around his neck. "This was the bestest day ever."

Meryl nodded and hugged him too. Josiah hugged them back, and after he'd untangled himself from their buttery fingers and stood, he studied the girls for a long time. His eyes appeared damp, but maybe it was only a trick of the light.

Then he straightened and stared off into a distance. His lips twisted, and his eyes grew shuttered. He'd blocked Lily out completely.

Josiah could barely speak around the lump blocking his throat. These precious girls should be part of his family, but how could he ever have a relationship with them? Leaving would be so hard. He could never forget them or Lily.

Lily herded the twins to the buggy. "*Danke* for all you've done for them."

"Don't thank me. Thank God." He deserved no praise. The gratefulness in Lily's expression made him squirm. He'd only just begun to pay down the gigantic debt he owed.

"We should go." He pulled two napkins he'd tucked in his coat pocket and wiped his nieces' faces. "What time is their mother expecting them?"

"I'm not sure. She got home around five this morning. I left a note telling her I'd watch her daughters while she slept. She'll probably sleep until noon or so."

In his joy at outfitting his nieces with necessities, he'd forgotten about avoiding Aliyah. They'd make it home before she awoke. Josiah breathed easier.

He'd drop everyone off, go back to the B and B to collect his things, and then call a driver to take him home. The thought depressed him.

By the time they pulled into the driveway, Meryl had fallen asleep. Scarlett's eyes drooped. They'd had a busy and exciting morning.

Josiah turned to Lily. "If you help Scarlett inside, I'll carry Meryl."

She nodded, but her eyes reflected his sadness. He'd hurt her by turning away. Yet, what else could he do? Cutting it off was for the best. Still, it didn't lessen the pain. How could he have gotten so entangled with two small girls and one lovely woman in such a short time?

CHAPTER 9

Josiah held the door open for Lily and, with his other arm, cuddled Meryl close to his chest. A picture flitted through his mind of him and Lily as parents, bringing their children inside after a family outing.

A sharp pain stabbed through him. That could never be. He'd been living a lie.

Aliyah came charging out of her house, screeching, "What are you doing with my children? Did I give you permission to take them anywhere?" Her words shot out like bullets, each one hitting Josiah in his gut.

But she hadn't been aiming her firepower at him. She hurtled toward Scarlett, and snatched her hand from Lily's. "What have you done to her?"

"She got a little sleepy on the ride home." Lily tried to soothe Aliyah, but the irate mother only scowled.

Then she whirled on Josiah. "Put my baby down this instant. How dare you—?" She froze in place as her gaze reached his face. Her mouth opened and closed, but no sound came out.

Josiah's arm tightened around Meryl. He wouldn't put her down. Not out here. She'd wake up disoriented. He'd set her on the couch.

All the color drained from Aliyah's cheeks. "You. . ." She sucked in a breath, and her whole body expanded like a mother bear ready to fight for her cub. "Give me my baby now," she thundered. "You have no rights to her. Not after abandoning me like that."

"What?" Lily's mouth gaped open. "You know each other?"

Josiah said *no*, as Aliyah said *yes*.

"You're a liar." She hissed her words out through clenched teeth.

"You've mistaken me for someone else."

"Oh, no I haven't. I'd know your face anywhere."

Her brow furrowed, Lily's gaze ping-ponged back and forth between them. Then, Scarlett swayed against her mother.

Lily reached out to support the little girl. "Let's go inside and put Scarlett down for a nap. Josiah can lay Meryl on the couch."

"Josiah?" Aliyah's bitter laugh carried a world of pain. "You lied to her about your name? Why? So you can get another woman in trouble?"

"You've made a mistake." He kept his words low and even. "My name really is Josiah."

LILY USHERED EVERYONE into the house and supervised putting the two children on the couch in the parlor. Then she stared at Aliyah and Josiah—if that was his real name—in confusion. What was going on here?

Eyes blazing, Aliyah leaned forward. She jutted her

pointer finger inches from his chest. "So, you just pretended your name was Simon?"

Lily sucked in a breath. *Simon?* Had her infatuation with this man blinded her to his lies? Was he the twins' father? The man who'd abandoned his children and their mother?

Part of Lily argued that the man who'd gently tucked the girls into blankets, bought them new clothes, and been kind to Martha would never do that. But he'd hidden the truth of his connection to Aliyah and the twins. That omission made Lily suspicious.

Josiah straightened to his full height, and Lily berated herself when her insides fluttered at his muscular shoulders, his take-charge attitude. He took two firm steps back from the finger Aliyah threatened to poke into his broad chest.

"I'm Simon's brother." Josiah's words fell with a thud.

Aliyah's face crumpled. Her shoulders slumped as the fight leaked out of her.

Lily's mind whirled. If he was related to Simon, why hadn't Josiah said so when she'd told him Aliyah's story? He'd only listened and sympathized. At least she'd assumed he'd been empathizing. He'd been very upset. At the time, she'd thought his reaction was caring. Maybe it had been guilt.

"Simon never knew about the babies. That's my fault."

Aliyah's eyes, narrow and assessing, studied Josiah. Lily did too. He'd been the cause of Aliyah's suffering?

"When you brought the letter, I worried it might change Simon's mind. The bishop and I wanted Simon to return the Amish community. I'd convinced him to go back with me that day. While Simon packed, I ripped the letter to shreds. Neither of us read it."

Aliyah sank into the nearest chair and covered her face with her hands.

Lily's heart went out to both of them. Josiah's story

cleared Simon of abandoning Aliyah. The whole situation had been a terrible and tragic misunderstanding.

As Josiah spoke, though, something else became clearer. He'd come into Lily's life under false pretenses. Lily had misinterpreted his interest in her. Josiah hadn't asked her home from the singing because he'd hoped to court her. He'd only wanted to find out about the twins.

The ache in her chest blossomed and spread throughout her body. She'd fallen for him when he had no romantic intentions. How could she have been such a fool?

Josiah cleared his throat. "After hearing about some of the things you and the girls have gone through, I want to do what I can to make things right. I can't give you those years back, but—"

"No, you can't." Aliyah lifted her head and shot him a fiery glare. "And you don't know even a tiny portion of what we lived through."

The lines etched into Josiah's face showed his anguish. "I'm sorry."

"And what are you doing here? Why didn't Simon come?"

"He, um, he's married and—"

"And he doesn't want people to know about his kids." Bitterness dripped from each one of Aliyah's words. "You Amish like to pretend you're goody-goodies, but you're no different from the rest of the world."

Josiah winced. "We sin and make many mistakes, and this is one of them."

"But you like to cover them up. Even if Simon had known, he'd have let me suffer to save his precious reputation."

"That's not true." But Josiah didn't sound too sure of his answer. "And now that we know," he said firmly, "I'll—I mean, we'll—take care of you and the children."

Aliyah angled her chin up. "A bribe for me to stay out of your lives? No, thanks. I don't want your money. I've made it this far without it. Just get out of here and leave me alone."

Josiah turned to Lily as if hoping she'd contradict Aliyah and ask him to stay. But right now, she couldn't deal with her jumbled feelings. She'd trusted him and even built up fantasies about courting him when he had no interest in her. He'd lied to her—maybe not outright, but he'd misled her by concealing the truth.

Lily lowered her lashes because she couldn't look at Josiah as she said the words she needed to say. Each one was wrenched from her. Each one tore off a piece of her heart. "Aliyah's right. You should go."

CHAPTER 10

Josiah had been expecting it, imagining it, dreading it. But when Lily uttered those words —*You should go*—with such finality, his heart squeezed into a tight, burning spot in his chest. The ache pulsed out from there, radiating to every part of his body.

He forced himself to move in mechanical steps to the front door. His throat had closed, but he managed one heartfelt, "I'm sorry," to both of them before he opened the door and strode out into the overcast day. A storm was brewing in the sky and in his life.

Each footfall away from Lily's front porch cut him more deeply. Over and over, he'd warned himself not to fall for her. But he hadn't followed his own advice. Somehow, this angelic woman had floated into his life. And now he'd never forget her sunny, welcoming smile. Her kindness and caring. Her gentle voice and bell-like laugh. Her womanly softness. Her love and generosity.

He'd allowed his emotions to sway his common sense. And he'd made not just one mistake, but two. Falling for her had been his first error, but lying to her had been worse.

Be sure your sins will find you out.

The change in her eyes—from adoration as he'd purchased the twins' clothing to revulsion as Simon's story unfolded—had been fitting punishment for his deception.

Josiah groaned. He'd covered up his real intentions to avoid facing her disappointment. But doing that had made everything much worse when the truth came out. If he'd told her before today, he would have tarnished her image of him. Now he'd not only done that, he'd also destroyed any chance of a relationship. Lily would never trust him again.

As much as he'd railed against getting involved with her, his attraction to her had overruled his good judgment. He'd lost his heart to her. And walking away now, he'd leave a huge piece of himself behind.

WHEN THE DOOR clicked shut behind Josiah with sharp finality, the floodgates inside Lily burst, and pain poured into her being, crashing through her in waves, washing away her hopes for the future, drowning her dreams.

"Are you all right?" Aliyah's gentle question penetrated Lily's self-pity.

Lily gripped the chair arms. *Lord, give me strength to cope.* "I will be." *With God's help.*

But now was not the time to focus on her own loss. She turned her attention to Aliyah, who'd been dealing with five years' worth of grief. Hearing the story of Simon had to have cut her deeply. "Does it help to know he didn't abandon you?"

"A little." Aliyah stared down at her lap. "All these years, I blamed Simon for my struggles and poverty. I told myself if he'd stayed, I'd have someone to help raise the girls, and we'd have a roof over our heads and. . ."

Lily waited quietly as Aliyah struggled with tears.

"I believed Simon was responsible for my loneliness, my grief, my exhaustion. But all along, I brought myself heartache by dwelling in the past. Now I know we wouldn't have made it as a couple. I'd never have agreed to become Amish."

"And I'm guessing Simon never would have left the community to become *Englisch*." Once his *Rumschpringa* ended, Lily suspected he'd have returned to his home and taken baptismal classes.

Aliyah nodded. "Back then, I'd rebelled against my strict upbringing and run away from home. I wanted nothing to do with God. Now I wonder if returning to the faith of my childhood would have made these struggles bearable."

"I'm sure it would have. God can comfort us through anything." Even losing someone she'd fallen for.

"Would you pray with me?" Aliyah leaned over and reached for Lily's hands. The checkbook Josiah had given Lily tumbled onto the floor, but Aliyah grasped Lily's fingers tightly, so she couldn't pick it up. "I've strayed so far from God, but I need to find my way back. I want to be an example for my children."

Lily prayed first, and Aliyah followed with a halting prayer of her own.

"Dear Lord Jesus, please forgive me for turning my back on you and living a life of sin. Please cleanse my soul of all disobedience, anger, and resentment. And from now on, help me to live a life that honors you."

When Aliyah lifted her head, her eyes shone with a new light. Lily thanked God for her neighbor's new commitment.

Silently, Lily prayed for her own situation. *Lord, please help me to accept Your will.*

Aliyah's sharp intake of breath drew Lily from her

tearful plea. Aliyah had picked up the checkbook and was staring at the open page, her mouth pursed into an *O*.

"What is it?" Lily leaned forward in concern as Aliyah held out the checkbook with shaking hands.

"It—it has my name on it."

Lily didn't want to intrude on the young mother's privacy but the clear, block-printed numbers stood out. Twenty thousand dollars? And Josiah planned to replenish it whenever it ran low?

"I—I don't know what to say." Aliyah hung her head. "I should have thanked him, but I don't have his address. I'm sorry I was so hasty in telling him to go."

"It was for the best," Lily murmured. Josiah's generosity choked her up, but she never wanted to face him again. Her feelings of betrayal were still raw. "I don't want to see him again."

Aliyah cocked one eyebrow. "I had a good reason for wanting him out of my life. But you?"

Lily bit her lip. Should she confess she'd fallen for him? *Nay*, it hurt too much to say the words. "He lied to me. When I told him about you and Simon, he acted as if he'd never heard the story before."

"He hadn't heard some of it." Aliyah swallowed hard. "He didn't know what the letter said. He didn't know about the babies."

True, but he still could have indicated Lily was describing his brother.

Shaking her head, Aliyah ran a hand over the checkbook cover. "I spent years stewing in anger and bitterness. And now, because of this money, I'm willing to forgive. What does that say about my character?"

"It says you just prayed for God's forgiveness, and that makes you willing to forgive others. You would have been fine with a small amount or even nothing at all, wouldn't you?"

The joy lighting Aliyah's face contrasted with Lily's low spirits. "You're right. And this money is a gift from God, not just Josiah. Although I am grateful for the part he played in giving it to me. I still can't believe this."

Then Aliyah's eyes lasered into Lily's. "And you? Have you forgiven him for lying to you?"

If Lily didn't answer truthfully, she couldn't criticize Josiah for lying. She lowered her head. "Not yet."

"I thought you Amish believed in forgiveness."

"We do. It's just that. . ." She couldn't put his betrayal in words. How did she explain it hurt her to know Josiah hadn't trusted her with the whole story? Did he see her as too judgmental and fear he couldn't share his brother's mistakes?

Lily replayed their conversations in her mind, trying to see if anything she'd said or done might have led him to that conclusion. And what had he said to mislead her?

He'd indicated he'd recently moved to this area. *Nay*, that wasn't true. She'd assumed that from his answers. He never came out and said he'd moved. After all, he was at a B and B. He hadn't bought a house or a farm. And when he said he'd come here on business, she presumed he meant landscaping. Instead, he'd been referring to Aliyah and the twins.

But he'd listened to her story about Aliyah without mentioning his part in it. Perhaps in keeping that to himself, he'd been trying to protect Aliyah's privacy. After all, Lily had just met him. Maybe she should give him the benefit of the doubt.

Aliyah studied Lily as she wrestled with her reluctance to let go. "Can't you ask God to give you a forgiving heart?"

Lily didn't answer right away because she had to admit other deeper truths. *Jah*, she could ask the Lord to soften her spirit. But part of her wanted to hang on to her anger at Josiah to avoid facing why she didn't want to forgive.

Josiah should have been honest with her about knowing Aliyah, but the real reason Lily wanted him out of her life had less to do with his actions than with her injured pride. She'd fallen hard for him, but realizing he didn't return her feelings had cut her deeply. She was too embarrassed to see him again.

Their ministers often warned against *hochmut*. And this was why. Her pride stood in the way of surrendering to God.

"Would it help if we prayed together?" Aliyah held out her hands again.

Lily tussled over keeping her secret to herself. But she confessed it to Aliyah, and they both bowed their heads as Lily asked God to take away her pride and shame.

When she opened her eyes, sun peeked through the clouds outside the window, and her spirits lightened. "I know where Josiah is staying. Should we get the girls and head over to see him?"

Aliyah nodded. "Yes, let's do that. I think we both have some apologizing to do."

CHAPTER 11

As soon as he returned to the B and B, Josiah packed his suitcase and checked out. Then he asked the Millers for the name of a driver to take him back to Gratz. They graciously called several drivers until they found one who was free.

Josiah paced back and forth past the pair of rocking chairs on the front porch while he waited. What was taking the man so long? All Josiah wanted to do was flee. He needed to get away from this area, from the memories haunting him.

He'd learned his lesson about lying. Until now, he'd always tried to be truthful. Except for lying to his brother. And misleading Lily. Both times he'd lied, he'd destroyed something precious.

A buggy pulled into the driveway, but Josiah was so immersed in his thoughts, he didn't look up. Instead, he glanced at his watch, impatient to be on his way.

"Josiahhhh!" two voices yelled.

His head jerked up. Scarlett and Meryl came racing toward him.

"How did you get here?" He prayed they'd come in the buggy that had pulled past the house. And that their driver had been their beautiful neighbor.

"Lily brought us."

Scarlett affirmed Josiah's hope. Maybe he'd get a chance to apologize to Lily. His pulse leaped as she rounded the corner with Aliyah. Unlike the frowns they'd both worn earlier, this time, they both grinned as they chatted. Would their cheerful expressions change once they spotted him?

Aliyah spoke first. "Lily brought me here so I could thank you."

Josiah's spirits plunged. Lily hadn't been coming to see him. Between sneaking peeks at her and trying to frame an apology, he barely heard Aliyah's speech of gratitude.

He tuned in when she described asking Jesus into her heart. "That's wonderful."

"I know." She beamed. "If only I'd done it years ago, I would have had God's help and strength during my trials."

Her words stabbed through him. "I'm so sorry you had to go through all that. I wish I hadn't lied to my brother. I should have given him the letter and trusted God for his future. Instead, I thought I knew best."

"What's done is done, and God used it to bring me back to Him. I suspect He also had another reason for it." She shot Lily a sideways smile. "Listen, I know you two need to talk, so I'll take the girls out back to look at the chickens and horses."

The girls had been competing to see who could rock the fastest. They jumped off the rocking chairs and scampered over to their mother.

"Yay!" Scarlett bounced up and down on her toes.

Meryl took her sister's hand. "We ain't never seen no real chickens."

"We never saw real chickens, Meryl," Aliyah said in a patient voice.

"I know. I said that."

Aliyah sighed and took Meryl's other hand. As she led her daughters away, Aliyah explained the finer points of grammar.

Lily smiled as she followed their progress across the lawn. How Josiah longed to stay in Bird-in-Hand so he could court her. But he'd ruined any chance of a relationship.

Still, he needed to make things right before he went. To break the awkward silence after Lily turned in his direction, he motioned to the rockers. "Want to sit?"

She sank into the closest rocker, but rather than relaxing, she wrung her hands, looking as if she'd rather be anywhere else but here. He might not have much time before she jumped up and hurried to join the twins.

He rushed to get the words out. "Lily, I'm so sorry I didn't tell you the truth about my brother and the real reason I came to Lancaster County. Will you forgive me?"

She avoided looking at him. All Amish been taught from childhood to forgive as God forgave, but Josiah didn't want a dutiful response. He longed for genuine forgiveness. Without it, he had no hope of a future friendship or—what he truly desired—a relationship.

Then she turned to face him. "Of course." The words rang with sincerity, and then her beautiful sunny smile lit up his world. He couldn't believe it.

To his surprise, she hung her head. In a voice so low he could barely hear it, she asked, "Will you forgive me for my unkindness and"—she nibbled at her lip and avoided his gaze—"and. . . my lie?"

"You didn't lie to me." Josiah couldn't picture Lily ever doing that.

"*Jah*, I did. Back at the house. I told you I wanted you to go. But I didn't."

Josiah's rocker squeaked to a stop. "You didn't?"

"*Nay*. And I wish you weren't leaving."

She sounded so miserable, he wanted to comfort her. If only he could pull her into his arms. He settled on reaching out a finger and tilting her chin so he could look into her eyes.

"If you want me to stay, I will. I can do my business from anywhere."

Her face lit with hope. "You can?"

"I'd do anything for you."

"That's because you have a generous heart. Look at all you've done for Aliyah and the twins."

"I wanted to make up for all their years of neglect. But I have different reason for doing things for you."

The eager light in her eyes gave him courage to tell her what was in his heart. "I fell for you after I met you, but I tried to talk myself out of it."

Her breathless "You did?" gave him hope.

But first he had to admit all the thoughts that had gone through his head. "I didn't see any future for us, especially not with Aliyah being your neighbor. And I'd misled you by pretending I didn't know her story. I assumed you'd never trust me again."

"I already forgave you. And it doesn't change how I feel about you."

Josiah swallowed hard before he asked the question burning inside. "How *do* you feel about me?"

"I fell for you too," she said shyly. "I hoped when you drove me home that night you intended to court me."

"I hurt you when I treated you so coldly, didn't I?"

Lily focused on her hands. "*Jah*."

"*Ach*, Lily, I'm so sorry. I never want to hurt you. Will you forgive me? And can we start over?"

She studied him for a moment. "Are you sure?"

"Very sure."

"Then *jah* and *jah*!"

Lily's enthusiastic agreement filled Josiah with more joy than he'd ever experienced. Not only had the sun overhead chased away all the clouds, Lily's glowing face made spring blossom in his heart and soul. He couldn't wait to plant the garden he and Lily would grow together—a garden of love, hope, and family. A garden where it would always be springtime in their hearts.

EPILOGUE

wo springs later. . .

Lily adjusted the black *kapp* on her head and smoothed down her white apron. Ten minutes to go until her wedding.

Loud footfalls pounded up the stairs, and the bedroom door burst open. Scarlett and Meryl bumped each other to be the first through the doorway.

Scarlett, looking sweet in a lilac Amish dress, beat her sister. "Guess what, Lily? I gots—got—to hold the new baby."

Not to be outdone, Meryl, in her favorite shade of pink, elbowed her sister aside. "I held Natty's hand and helped him walk."

"He already knows how." Scarlett's tone held a sarcastic edge.

Meryl glared. "He don't—doesn't--walk too good yet. Katie said he needs help 'cos he's only eighteen months old."

Smiling, Lily bent to hug them. "I'm sure you're both a big help to Katie."

Simon had confessed everything to his wife, and true to her sweet nature, Katie had quickly forgiven him and grown to love the twins. Some weekends, the girls went to stay with Simon and Katie.

Scarlett and Meryl had fallen head over heels in love with their baby brother, Natty, when he was born that first October. Then Katie and Simon had another boy a few months ago. The twins loved spending time with their *daed*, Katie, and the little boys.

Their weekends away gave Aliyah time for her acting. She'd starred in several productions at Sight and Sound. During her weekday rehearsals, the girls stayed with Lily. Some nights, the twins slept over.

Not only had Aliyah reversed her dislike of the Amish, she even allowed Lily to take the girls to church, and Aliyah sent them to the Amish school nearby. She agreed they should learn about their father's faith. On off-Sundays, she took them to her church.

Josiah had purchased the property near Lily for Aliyah, and he'd helped the men of the *g'may* rebuild the house, expanding and modernizing it. He'd also done the landscaping, while Lily helped the girls plant a garden.

Lily still smiled when she recalled the first time Scarlett and Meryl had seen the tomato flowers in her garden that first summer. They'd squealed and waited impatiently for the tomatoes.

"You was right," Meryl crowed the day they'd picked the first one. "'Matoes really do grow on them skinny green stems."

"We has to plant our own garden," Scarlett insisted. She'd been disappointed to learn she'd have to wait until the following year to grow her own tomatoes.

Now, though, the two girls had become seasoned gardeners. They also helped Lily and Katie in their gardens.

Scarlett frowned at Lily's blue dress and white apron. "When you gonna get dressed? Mommy says the wedding's starting soon."

"I am dressed." Lily twirled around so they could see the new dress she'd sewn.

Scarlett looked horrified. "You can't wear that. Where's your white gown?"

Meryl's brow knotted. "And yer veil?"

"That's only for *Englisch* weddings. This is for Amish weddings."

"Lily still looks pretty, doesn't she, Scarlett?" Meryl studied Lily with an anxious look on her face, then she leaned over to whisper in her sister's ear. "We don't want to hurt her feelings. 'Member what Mommy says about being nice to everyone."

"I am being nice. I'm helping Lily look better for her wedding."

Martha peeked into the room, interrupting Meryl's loud huff. "*Ach*, Lily, you look beautiful!"

"See," Meryl said to Scarlett, "that's what yer supposed to say to brides."

A rapturous look in her eyes, Martha wrapped her arms around herself. "I'm so excited to be a side-sitter. *Danke*, *Danke*, Lily!"

"I'm so glad you're doing it." Lily and Josiah had both agreed Martha should have a special place in their wedding. "You were with us on our first date."

"I know. I told you Josiah would marry you, didn't I? And I was right!"

"Jah, you were." How embarrassed Lily had been that night. She'd worried about Josiah overhearing Martha's comments. If only Lily had known what the future held. . .

"We need to head downstairs. It's almost eight," Martha warned. She ushered Scarlett and Meryl ahead of her. "Your *mamm* is waiting for you two."

The girls skedaddled down the steps, and Martha followed more sedately.

The next time Lily saw all three of them, she'd be a married woman. Married to the man she loved with all her heart.

MARTHA'S GRIN stretched from ear to ear as Josiah, with Lily at his side, made his way to the *eck*, the special corner table that had been beautifully decorated. Josiah's smile most likely matched Martha's because his whole being overflowed with love and joy for his beloved. His dreams had come true today as he'd made his promises before God to take Lily as his wife.

After they sat in their places, Josiah twined his fingers through Lily's under the table. Then he leaned past his beautiful bride to speak to Martha.

"*Danke* for being here with us today. You've been a part of the two most special days of our lives. We might not have met if it weren't for you."

"I know." Martha beamed with pride. "That night, I told Lily you would marry her."

Lily laughed. "I didn't believe you, and I don't think Josiah did either. Neither of us could have guessed what God had planned."

When her eyes met his, Josiah tried to convey all the tenderness and deep love he felt for his sweet wife. "We never know what blessings God has in store for us. And you are the most *wunderbar* blessing I've ever received after God's love and forgiveness."

Lily sniffled and dabbed at her eyes.

Alarmed, Josiah stared at her. "Are you crying?"

"Don't worry. They're tears of joy. I'm so grateful to God for bringing you into my life. Two years ago, I'd hit a low point. I was missing *Mamm* and regretting that I'd be an *alt maedel.*"

"You?" Josiah couldn't believe it. A woman as beautiful, sweet, caring, kind. . . His list could go on and on.

"*Jah.* I remember tucking the twins in when they stayed overnight and thinking God had brought them into my life to make up for me not having a family."

"They are your family now, but we'll have some little ones of our own too."

Her watery smile revealed she wanted children as much as he did. He marveled that God had given him such a perfect helpmeet.

Thomas King passed the table and winked at Josiah. "Told you Lily was right pretty and had a good heart. You believe me now?"

"I've always agreed with you." Josiah had guessed it that day, and now he knew it for sure and certain. He'd married the most wonderful woman in the *g'may.* His heart overflowed with gratitude.

"I hope you and Lily will be as happy as Mae and I are after fifty-seven years."

Lily squeezed Josiah's hand under the table and smiled at Thomas. "I hope so too."

"Well, if you keep God at the center of your union, you will be. Now I want to join my blushing bride." With a quick wave, Thomas headed off to join the gray-haired woman who still looked at him with stars in her eyes as if they were newlyweds.

"I want us to be as in love as they are when we're that age," Lily whispered.

"We will be. We'll put God first in our marriage." For the next fifty-seven springs—or however many years the good Lord gave them—Josiah would always see Lily as his blushing bride. And if he loved her the way the Bible commanded, he knew in his heart, she'd still look at him with the same adoration as she did today. And like Thomas and his wife, Josiah prayed he and Lily would go on to be an example to other couples.

THANK YOU

FOR READING THIS BOOK

I'm grateful you chose it, and I pray the story blessed and uplifted you.

If you enjoyed the story,
you can make a big difference.

Honest reviews are extremely important to authors. They bring our books to the attention of other readers.

If you liked the book, I'd be grateful if you could spend a few minutes leaving a review.

Thank you ever so much!

Rachel

P.S. If you'd enjoy learning more about the Amish, please join my private Facebook group, the Hitching Post: https://www.facebook.com/groups/196506777789849/

And if you haven't already, you can sign up for my newsletter at http://bit.ly/1qwci4Q

ABOUT THE AUTHOR

USA Today bestselling author Rachel J. Good writes life-changing, heart-tugging novels of faith, hope, and forgiveness. She grew up near Lancaster County, Pennsylvania, the setting for her Amish novels. Striving to be as authentic as possible, she spends time with her Amish friends, doing chores on their farm and attending family events.

Rachel is the author of several Amish series in print or forthcoming – the bestselling *Love & Promises*, *Sisters & Friends*, *Unexpected Amish Blessings*, *Green Valley Farmer's Market and Auction* (2021), and two books in *Hearts of Amish Country* – as well as the *Amish Quilts Coloring Books*. In addition, she has stories in many anthologies, including *Amish Christmas Twins* and *Christmas at the Amish Bakeshop* with Shelley Shepard Gray and Loree Lough. She is also the coauthor of the *Prayerful Author Journey: Inspirational Weekly Planner*.

Rachel hosts the Hitching Post, an online site where she shares Amish information and her book research. She also enjoys meeting readers in person and speaks regularly at book events, schools, libraries, churches, book clubs, and conferences across the country. Find out more about her at: www.racheljgood.com

ALSO BY RACHEL J. GOOD

HAVE YOU READ THEM ALL?

SISTERS & FRIENDS series

Change of Heart

When her younger sister goes wild during *Rumschpringa* and dates an *Englischer*, Lydia Esh teams up with his older brother to break up the couple. But she doesn't count on falling for an *Englischer* herself. Will Lydia stay true to her faith if it means giving up the man she loves?

Buried Secrets

Emma Esh has recovered physically from the accident that almost claimed her life, but she has no memory of the year before the accident, so she has no idea why her sister tries to keep her from falling in love with their next-door neighbor Sam Troyer. But an unexpected visit from an old boyfriend and the gradual return of her memory tears Emma's life and romance apart.

Gift from Above

Sarah Esh's peaceful life is torn apart when a parachutist crash-lands on her family farm and begs her to keep his presence secret because his life's in danger. That promise tangles her in a web of deceit that endangers innocent people, ruins her best friend's reputation, and tears apart the Amish community. Sarah must confess and repair the damage she's done, but how can she admit the truth to Jakob Zook, knowing it will end their relationship?

Big-City Amish

After Abner Lapp's betrayal and his choice to leave the Amish community, Rebecca Zook tries to forget him, but how can she ignore his mother's plea to watch his four young brothers during her cancer treatments in New York City, even if it means being around Abner? Rebecca's tender heart won't allow her to ignore him when he's hurting, but she can't let herself fall for him again, especially when he's not right with God.

LOVE & PROMISES series

The Amish Teacher's Gift

A teacher at the Amish school for children with special needs, Ada Rupp struggles to balance her job with caring for her seven orphaned siblings. She has no time to date, but she'll do anything in her power to help her young student, Nathan Yoder, and his grieving widowed father.

The Amish Midwife's Secret

When Amish midwife Leah Stoltzfus insists on using herbal remedies for her patients, sparks fly between her and the new *Englischer* doctor, Kyle Miller. In more ways than one. Can they overcome their differences to rescue a pregnant teen and save her unborn baby?

The Amish Widow's Rescue

After Grace Fisher's husband dies unexpectedly, her neighbor, the reclusive Elijah Beiler, offers to help with her animals and household repairs just to be neighborly. He has no intention of getting entangled with the pregnant widow or her children; he's been hurt enough in the past. But he hasn't counted on Grace's young son, who's determined they need a new daddy.

UNEXPECTED AMISH BLESSINGS series

His Unexpected Amish Twins

When Micah Miller becomes the guardian of his twin niece and nephew after their parents are killed in a buggy accident, he's grateful for Hope Graber, owner of a horse therapy farm, who helps all three of them all deal with their grief. Hope makes them smile again and wins a place in Micah's heart. But will his deep-seated fears and Hope's close partnership with her *Englisch* trainer keep them apart?

His Pretend Amish Bride

Priscilla Ebersol has no chance of marriage after her boyfriend's humiliating rejection ruins her reputation, but after she helps an Amish camel farmer in a nearby town and she's mistaken for his wife, Priscilla's matchmaking *mamm* sees this as the perfect opportunity. Unfortunately, her meddling might drive the couple apart instead of together.

His Accidental Amish Family

Following a buggy accident, Anna Flaud is told she'll

never walk again. She refuses to accept that and spends years recovering, and she's also working toward becoming a foster parent. Then she's offered a chance to fulfill her dearest wish —motherhood—by adopting three siblings with special needs. But it comes with strings attached: she needs a husband. Her exercise therapist, Levi King, would be perfect for the role except Levi can't trust himself to care for one child, let along three.

SURPRISED BY LOVE series

Unexpected Amish Proposal

After Fern Blauch loses her market stall, Gideon Hartzler offers to share his stand with her, but once they start working together, will her rival in business end up as a rival for her heart?

Unexpected Amish Courtship

Isaac Lantz, who trains Labrador retrievers as guide dogs, is enamored with Sovilla Mast, who sells homemade dog food and treats. Gaining a dog's affection is easy, but bashful Isaac has no idea how to win the heart of the woman he loves.

Unexpected Amish Christmas

To help himself recover after a buggy accident, Jeremiah Zook pens inspirational letters to grieving families mentioned in the Amish newspaper. Moved by the letter he's sent, Keturah Esch corresponds with him. Little does she know, Jeremiah has a nearby market stand. When he shows interest in her, she rebuffs him because her heart belongs to the anonymous letter writer. A Christmas gift accompanied by a letter might just hold the key to both their hearts' desires.

Amish Marriage of Convenience

When widower Stephen Lapp moves his five children from New York State to Lancaster County, Pennsylvania, his only plan is to buy his family's farm stand. But on Stephen's first trip to the market, his brave act of kindness nearly ends in catastrophe—until strong-willed Nettie Hartzler saves him—and makes an impression he can't forget. Nettie has no interest in getting involved with any man. But when Nettie runs into serious money worries and Stephen proposes a marriage of convenience, she's distressed and conflicted. She's come to know Stephen's gentle heart and generous soul, but will he marry her if she reveals her dark past?

Her Pretend Amish Boyfriend

Noah Riehl has dark secrets in his past that prevent him from marrying a faith-centered Amish girl like Caroline Hartzler. But when she needs a fake boyfriend to discourage a persistent suitor, who won't take no for an answer, he agrees to rescue her. But will his kindness lead him into the very relationship he's vowed to avoid?

Dating an Amish Flirt

Everyone accuses Rachel Glick of being a flirt because she's caused several breakups and broke many hearts, but she only wants to spend time with her brother's friends after his death. Josh Yoder wants to help the grieving family, and God seems to be leading him to Rachel. But with her history of breaking hearts, is she the right choice?

Missing Her Amish Boyfriend

Anna Mary Zook is struggling to cope with her new job at the market and care for her five younger siblings as Mamm spirals into another depression. Abe King longs to be there for her, but he can't leave his aging father to run their New York state farm alone. Can Abe and Anna Mary find a way to be together?

Amish Second-Chance Romance

When Cathy Zehr asks crusty bachelor Myron King for advice on single parenting, he's shocked because he failed while raising his rebellious nephew. Her sharp-tongued response—knowing what he did wrong might help her avoid the same mistakes—makes him wonder if he's being given a second chance at parenting. And love.

ROMANTIC SUSPENSE NOVELLAS

AMISH HOMETOWN HEROES series

Amish men face danger and intrigue to protect the ones they love. Can they trust God, their instincts, and their hearts?

Amish Secret Identity

When an *Englisher* pays Marty an exorbitant fee for yard work, he's wary. He's even more shocked when she offers him even more money to turn her granddaughter Amish. He refuses, but when Olivia and her grandmother both end up missing, Marty is fingered for the crime because he was the last one to see them alive.

Amish Undercover Deception

Crist Petersheim blames God for the tragedies in his life, so the last thing he wants is to get involved with an Amish girl. But he fears for Faithe Beiler's safety when she invites every homeless person in the neighborhood, including drug dealers and criminals, to a free Thanksgiving dinner. Street savvy, Crist risks his life to protect her from danger. But can he protect his heart?

AMISH DETECTIVE BENUEL MILLER series

Mysteries intrigue shop owner Benuel Miller. Although strangers may think a blind man will be easy to cheat, criminals who think he can't identify them soon find out they're wrong—dead wrong.

Amish Twin Trouble

When two twin sisters enter his shop, Benuel senses trouble. His hunches have never led him astray, but is he misreading something here? He can't help being drawn to Mari. Yet is she as sweet and loving as she seems? Or is she hiding a deep, dark secret?

Amish Wedding Day Revenge

An escaped convict bent on revenge interrupts Mari's marriage preparations. She has no idea she's in for the most harrowing experience of her life. Her beloved, Benuel, is a detective, but can she leave clues he can find? Or will she never see him again?

Missing Amish Daughter

When Benuel Miller's daughter, Susanna, return home after school one day, he starts a harrowing search, but she's disappeared without a trace. For Susanna, the nightmare has only begun. Can she escape? Or will she end up dead?

Amish Detective Benuel Miller Collection

Read all three stories in one volume: *Amish Twin Trouble*, *Amish Wedding Day Revenge*, and *Missing Amish Daughter*.

ANTHOLOGIES

Amish Christmas Twins*, *Christmas at the Amish Bakeshop*, *The Christmas Gathering (with Shelley Shepard Gray and Loree Lough)

Amish Christmas Kinner (with Lenora Worth and Kelly Long)

Amish Christmas Miracles*, *More Amish Christmas Miracles*, *Amish Spring Romance (with Jennifer Beckstrand, Jennifer Spredemann, and others)

Amish Across America (free; with multiple authors)

Amish Christmas Cookie Tours*, *An Amish Christmas Table (with Mindy Steele and Jennifer Beckstrand)

Love's Truest Hope (with Mary Alford and Laura V. Hilton)

Love's Thankful Heart*, *Plain Everyday Heroes*, *Love's Christmas Blessings
(with Laura V. Hilton and/or Thomas Nye)

ROMANCE NOVELLAS

Amish Christmas Treasure
Amish Mistletoe & Miracles

Spring Blossoms in Amish Country

OTHER TITLES

Amish Quilts Coloring Book (regular and large-print versions)

Prayerful Author Journey: Inspirational Weekly Planner

Hearts Reunited in ***Hearts of Amish Country series***

Love's Secret Identity in ***Hearts of Amish Country series***

Check for more Rachel J. Good titles here.

Made in the USA
Monee, IL
28 July 2025

22021705R00059